LOOKS LIKE WAR

"Did I hear right?" Veronica demanded. "Is that obnoxious royal pain actually coming here for a visit?"

"If you're referring to Tessa," Lisa replied coolly, "then the answer is yes. And I'm sure she's just dying to see you, too."

"Like I care what she thinks," Veronica snapped huffily. She whirled around and stormed back to Danny's stall.

"Uh-oh," Carole whispered. "It looks like you were right, Lisa. Veronica is holding a major grudge against Tessa. I guess she's mad that Tessa didn't recognize her superior breeding and introduce her to the queen."

Stevie rubbed her hands together. "Uh-huh," she agreed. "This could be trouble. We'll have to figure out the best way to handle it so that—"

"Stop right there, Stevie," Lisa interrupted. "In case you've already forgotten, we can't 'handle' anything right now. At least not the way you're thinking."

Carole nodded emphatically. "Lisa's right," she said. "Max is really mad this time. And the worst part is, Veronica knows it. If we do anything to her . . ."

THE SADDLE CLUB

ENGLISH HORSE

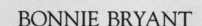

BONNIE BRYANT

A SKYLARK BOOK
NEW YORK • TORONTO • LONDON • SYDNEY • AUCKLAND

RL 5, 009–012

ENGLISH HORSE

A Bantam Skylark Book / July 1998

ISBN 0-553-48629-2

Published simultaneously in the United States and Canada.

PRINTED IN THE UNITED STATES OF AMERICA

OPM   0 9 8 7 6 5 4 3 2 1

*I would like to express my special thanks
to Catherine Hapka for her help
in the writing of this book.*

"SHE'LL BE SORRY," Stevie Lake muttered, tossing the water balloon she was holding from hand to hand.

Stevie's two best friends, Carole Hanson and Lisa Atwood, exchanged glances in the dusty, mottled sunlight pouring through the high windows of the hayloft at Pine Hollow Stables. They didn't have to ask whom Stevie was talking about. They knew. The "she" in question was Veronica diAngelo, a fellow rider at Pine Hollow and a middle-school classmate of Stevie's.

"I'm still not sure this is a good idea." Lisa gingerly shifted her own water balloon from one hand to the other and peeked over the side of the loft at the empty stable aisle below. "What if Max finds out? You know how he hates horseplay in the stable."

Carole giggled. "From us humans, at least. For some reason he doesn't seem to mind it as much from the horses."

Lisa laughed, too. But she was still worried. Veronica diAngelo was an incurable snob who thought her family's wealth made her better than everyone else, and Lisa didn't like her any more than Stevie did. But she was afraid that Stevie's water balloon scheme might get them in trouble with Max Regnery, the owner of Pine Hollow and the girls' riding instructor.

Stevie shrugged. "Don't worry about Max," she said breezily. "I overheard him on the phone while I was filling the balloons, and it sounded like he was busy lining up some new boarders or something. He'll probably be stuck in the office for hours filling out paperwork and boring stuff like that." She glanced down at the bucket beside her. Normally the bright blue plastic flat-back bucket could be found hanging in the stall of Stevie's horse, Belle, filled with fresh drinking water. However, at the moment it was filled with water balloons. "And that should give us plenty of time to teach Veronica why she shouldn't mess with me," she added with grim satisfaction.

Carole rolled her eyes. "Come on, Stevie." She wiped a trickle of sweat off her forehead. It was only June, but the afternoons in Willow Creek, Virginia, were already hot and muggy. "If anyone but Veronica had played that prank on you, you would've loved it."

Lisa winced as Stevie glared at Carole. She knew that Carole was right. But she also knew that Stevie's famous sense of humor sometimes deserted her when it came to Veronica.

Stevie and Veronica both attended a private school called Fenton Hall, which was located across town from Carole and Lisa's public school. On the last day of classes a week earlier, Fenton Hall had held its annual awards ceremony. This year the presenter had been Ms. Haines, a retiring English teacher who was rumored to be half senile. Veronica had arranged for the elderly teacher to present Stevie with a very special award—for best dressed boy. Ms. Haines had proudly called Stevie up onto the stage of the packed auditorium to accept her "trophy," which consisted of a hideous plaid necktie displayed in an elaborate gold frame.

"I still can't believe Veronica convinced Ms. Haines that that stupid award was for real," Stevie muttered under her breath.

Lisa noticed that Stevie was squeezing her water balloon rather tightly. In fact, the balloon was in danger of bursting and soaking them all. Lisa moved a few inches away. "Um," she said tentatively, "are you sure this water balloon thing is really the best way to get back at Veronica?"

"Are you kidding?" Stevie frowned. "This is just the beginning. Sort of like a warning shot. I mean, you must admit, *she* started it this time. I may have played a few tiny pranks on Veronica in the past, but that didn't give her the right to humiliate me in front of my entire school." Stevie loosened her grip on the water balloon and flopped down on her stomach, sending stray wisps of hay and dust flying. "This time she's going to pay. Big time."

Carole and Lisa looked at each other again. Both of them knew that there was no point in trying to reason with their friend when she used that tone of voice. Stevie was definitely the most headstrong of the three girls, as well as the most wacky and mischievous. Those qualities made her very interesting to be around. And whenever her strong personality got her into hot water, Carole and Lisa were always there to help her out. That was one of the reasons they had formed The Saddle Club. The group had only two rules: Members had to be horse-crazy, and they had to be willing to help each other whenever help was needed. Sometimes the second rule meant offering assistance with riding or homework or family problems. Other times it meant pitching in to wreak horrible revenge on Veronica—at least that was how Stevie felt about it.

Stevie wriggled forward a few more inches until her shoulders cleared the edge of the loft. From that vantage point, she could see into the stalls of several of the stable's horses, including Veronica's sleek Thoroughbred gelding, Danny. More important, she had a good view of the aisle in front of the stalls.

"We should each be able to get off at least two or three rounds before she realizes what's happening," she mused. She reached over and grabbed another water balloon. "Maybe more if we work really fast."

Carole slid forward next to Stevie and peered over the edge. "We're lucky Max switched the stall assignments around when the new horses arrived last month: Danny isn't stabled near Rusty or Geronimo anymore," she remarked. "Otherwise we wouldn't be able to do this. We all know how spooky Rusty can sometimes be about water, and Geronimo is too hyper to tolerate *anything* falling into his stall."

"Hmmm," Stevie replied. "By the way, did you notice how we're only using red, white, and blue water balloons? I did that as a silent protest against the way Veronica has been bragging about giving the opening remarks at the country club on July Fourth weekend."

Lisa hid a smile. She had the funniest feeling that Stevie was changing the subject because the idea of her water balloons upsetting the horses hadn't even occurred to her. Naturally, though, Carole had seen the potential problem right away. That was typical of both Lisa's friends. Stevie tended to get so caught up in her schemes and pranks that she sometimes forgot about everything else. Carole could be even more scatterbrained than Stevie, but never when it came to horses. For her, horses always came first, second, and third, making her easily the horse-craziest of the three horse-crazy girls.

"Speaking of the Fourth of July," Lisa said, "whoever thought that anything good would come out of my parents' finally being accepted into the Willow Creek Country Club?"

"I know," Stevie said. "I still can't believe it was your mother's idea to hold a day of point-to-point races that weekend."

Lisa grimaced. "Actually, I think it was inspired by Mrs. diAngelo. They're cochairs of the fund-raising committee, and my mom has been a lot more excited about horses since she started chatting with Mrs. diAngelo about Veronica and Pine Hollow and Danny." She shrugged. "But you have to admit, whoever's idea it was, it should be a lot of fun. I've never even seen a point-to-point before, let alone ridden in one."

"Neither have I," Stevie admitted. She sat up to say more, still balancing a water balloon in each hand. "What's the difference between a point-to-point and a steeplechase again?" She had been just as thrilled as her friends to hear about the upcoming equestrian event, which would take place on the Saturday before Independence Day. Mrs. Atwood had been steadily planning for more than a month, but lately Stevie had been so busy formulating her revenge against Veronica that she hadn't paid much attention to the details. She knew a little bit about steeplechasing, which was a form of horse racing that included jumps. But she wasn't clear on the difference between that and what was happening at the country club in a couple of weeks.

"They're really pretty similar," said Carole, who loved sharing her knowledge about horses. "Both involve races over a course that includes jumps. A point-to-point usually takes place cross-country instead of at a racetrack, but otherwise I think it's pretty much just the amateur version of the professional sport."

"I've seen a couple of steeplechase races on TV," Lisa said, "like that famous one in England. . . . What's it called again?"

"The Grand National?" Stevie offered. Lisa nodded, and Stevie smiled. "I've seen that one on TV, too. It's pretty exciting, isn't it?"

Lisa shifted her water balloon back to her other hand. "It's definitely exciting," she agreed. "But maybe a little scary, too. All those horses and jockeys racing full speed over those big jumps . . ."

"I know what you mean," Carole said. "That's why I'm glad Max is involved with the country club event. He'll make sure everybody follows the rules and keeps things as safe as possible."

Stevie giggled. "I still can't picture Max sitting through a committee meeting with all those country club members."

The others laughed, too. It *was* hard to imagine their down-to-earth, no-nonsense riding instructor sipping tea and making small talk with Mrs. Atwood, Mrs. diAngelo, and the other ladies of the club. But they were all glad that the fund-raising committee had invited Max to be one of their expert advisers.

At that moment, somewhere below the three girls, a horse let out a loud snort. Lisa glanced down and saw a handsome chestnut gelding tossing his head restlessly. "It looks like Derby is a little restless," she commented. "I guess he's still getting used to his new home."

Carole followed her gaze. "Isn't he amazing?" she said, her voice filling with admiration as she watched the spirited, reddish gold horse. "He's half Holsteiner and half Thoroughbred, so he'll be a really good all-around horse for the more advanced riders here. I think Max is really pleased with him. The other new horses, too."

Lisa rested her chin on her hand and watched the big gelding for a moment. Derby was one of three horses Max had bought recently from a dealer in England. "I wonder if anyone will be riding him in the point-to-point," she said idly. Then she smiled. "Can you believe the point-to-point is only a couple of weeks away? I wouldn't believe it myself if I hadn't been helping Mom with the planning for ages already."

Carole grinned. "It's going to be incredible. Not even Veronica's opening remarks will be able to spoil it." Because her mother was the head of the fund-raising committee and a longtime member of the country club, Veronica had managed to get herself invited to give a speech at the beginning of the big day's events. She hadn't stopped bragging about it since it was settled.

"I have to hand it to your mother, Lisa. The point-to-point is probably the most exciting news to hit this place in ages," Stevie said happily.

"The *second* most exciting news," Lisa corrected. "The *most* exciting news is Tessa's visit."

Stevie nodded. "I stand—I mean, sit—corrected," she said.

Lisa had first met Lady Theresa, known to her friends as Tessa, during a family trip to England. The two girls had hit it off immediately, and Lisa had discovered that Tessa was just as horse-crazy as she was. Later, when Lisa, Carole, and Stevie had traveled to England to participate in a Pony Club event, the foursome got along royally, and at the end of the visit they had made her an official out-of-town member of The Saddle Club. Now Tessa was finally coming to visit her American friends. She was arriving that night and staying with Lisa's family for about two weeks.

"I just thought of something." Stevie held up the balloons in her hand. "Maybe we should have waited one more day to make Veronica pay for her crimes against humanity. I bet Tessa would have loved to help out. Remember how much fun we all had in England when we tricked Veronica into thinking she'd found those long lost royal jewels?"

Lisa remembered. She also remembered how angry Veronica had been about their prank. "You know, I think we might want to keep Tessa and Veronica away from each other as much as possible," she said. "Veronica was pretty mad at us about that whole incident, but I think she was even madder at Tessa. You know, because Tessa's distantly related to the queen of England and Veronica thinks that's terribly important."

Carole nodded. "You're probably right. Veronica has some weird ideas about how different people are supposed to act, and she can be—"

"Shhh!" Stevie hissed. "I hear footsteps. Prepare to attack!"

Lisa sighed, then hunched down beside Stevie, her water balloon at the ready. The footsteps were coming from the section of the aisle directly below the loft, so the girls couldn't see who was coming. "Are you sure it's Veronica?" she whispered.

Stevie nodded. "Hardly anyone else is around," she whispered back. "Besides, I saw Veronica in the locker room before we came up here. She said she was going for a trail ride." She leaned forward a few more inches. "Get ready," she whispered. "She's almost here."

Lisa caught one glimpse of a tweed jacket. That was all she had time to take in before Stevie exploded into action beside her.

"Fire!" Stevie howled, hurling her water balloons downward.

Lisa dropped her first balloon and reached for another,

10

her hand bumping into Carole's in the bucket. Stevie's arms were a whirl of motion as she fired balloon after balloon into the aisle below. Angry and bewildered voices rose up toward the three girls.

Lisa dropped her second balloon, then paused with a frown. *Voices? Wait a minute . . .* Two more figures stepped into sight, dripping wet. Lisa gasped as the woman in the tweed jacket looked up, her deeply lined face looking startled.

They had attacked the wrong target!

"Uh-oh," Stevie murmured as she, too, realized their mistake.

The three people standing in the aisle below were staring up at the girls in the loft with a variety of expressions on their faces. The aristocratic-looking elderly woman in the tweed jacket still looked startled. The handsome, dark-haired teenage boy beside her looked confused and annoyed. Max Regnery looked downright furious. But despite their different reactions, the three victims of the misdirected prank did have one thing in common: They were all sopping wet.

"Stephanie Lake!" Max bellowed, pointing a finger at Stevie, who was still leaning over the edge of the loft. "Get down here this instant."

12

" 'Uh-oh' is right," Lisa whispered to Carole. "We'd better get down there, too."

The three girls climbed down from the loft and faced the glowering Max. "Um, s-sorry about that," Stevie stammered. "We thought you were someone else."

Max didn't answer her. He turned to face his two companions. "I don't even know how to begin to apologize for this, Mrs. Pennington." His voice, while carefully controlled, was shaking slightly with anger. "And to you, Miles, of course. I assure you both, this sort of thing doesn't normally happen here at Pine Hollow." He shot The Saddle Club a stern glance. "And I can assure you that I will be looking into it immediately."

Carole gulped. Max looked just about as furious as she had ever seen him.

"It's quite all right, Mr. Regnery," the old woman said politely. She brushed a few drops of water off of her jacket and ran one hand through her damp, wavy gray hair. "A little water never hurt anyone. Isn't that right, Miles?"

The teenager managed a weak grin. "Right, Grandmother," he agreed. He tried to shake some of the water out of his cotton polo shirt but only succeeded in getting his grandmother even wetter. He turned toward Max. "Um, is there somewhere we could mop up?" Lisa noticed that the boy had a somewhat stiff and formal way of speaking. She wondered if that was natural or if it had something to do with the cold water dripping down his back.

"Certainly," Max said through clenched teeth. "Let me show you to the washroom." He started down the aisle after the Penningtons, then paused for a moment beside The Saddle Club. "Don't move," he ordered quietly. Then he hurried away without a backward glance.

The three girls were silent for a moment. Finally Stevie spoke up. "Wow. Max looked pretty mad."

Lisa shook her head grimly. "I think 'mad' is an understatement."

They didn't have time to discuss it any further. Max came hurrying back down the aisle toward them. Stevie opened her mouth to start apologizing again, but Max didn't give her a chance. "What in the name of all that is decent in this world did you girls think you were doing?" he shouted. His face was rapidly turning a bright shade of magenta, and a vein in his forehead was starting to throb.

"Um, sorry?" Stevie said meekly. "We were just . . . um . . ." She searched for the best way to explain. Somehow, now that she thought about it, she didn't think that an explanation like "We wanted to get revenge on Veronica for making me look stupid in school" would get them very far.

"Sorry!" Max barked. "Is that all you have to say?" He roughly ran a hand through his hair, making it stand straight up in tufts.

Carole bit her lip to keep from laughing at the sight. "But we really are sorry, Max," she said. "And you don't have to worry—we were already planning to pick up all

14

the balloon pieces so that none of the horses would swallow them."

"Gee," Max said, sounding very sarcastic. "That was thoughtful of you."

Carole blushed, and the other two girls exchanged desperate glances. Stevie was still trying to figure out how to talk their way out of this one. She wasn't used to The Saddle Club being the target of Max's genuine wrath. Usually that honor was reserved for Veronica, who was always making Max angry with her carelessness and laziness.

"What's all the noise out here?" a familiar voice came from behind them. "You're going to scare Danny."

Stevie turned and saw Veronica coming down the aisle, Danny's saddle in her arms. Max glanced over his shoulder at her.

"Never mind, Veronica," he said sternly. "This doesn't concern you."

Veronica's eyes narrowed. She glanced from Max to Stevie and back again. Her curious gaze took in Carole's and Lisa's downcast faces, too. "Fine," she said, a little too casually. "I'm no busybody." She took a few more steps down the aisle. "Well, I'll be in Danny's stall if anybody needs me. I want to give him a good grooming before I tack him up."

Stevie scowled. Veronica was famous for never doing her stable chores herself. She liked to think of Red O'Malley, Pine Hollow's head stable hand, as her personal servant. Stevie was positive that Veronica had been on her way to find Red so that she could dump the task of tacking up onto the hardworking young man. And she was equally sure that Veronica had absolutely no intention of leaving the immediate area before she spent some quality time eavesdropping on Max and The Saddle Club.

Max didn't seem to realize what Veronica was up to, though—or if he did, he didn't care. "Mrs. Pennington will never board her horses here now," he muttered. He seemed to be talking more to himself than to the girls.

"She's boarding some horses here?" Carole asked eagerly. Despite the trouble they were in, she couldn't help feeling excited that there would be more newcomers to Pine Hollow. "What kind of horses? How many?"

Max didn't answer. He just glared. "She *was* thinking of boarding here," he said icily. "But that was before she encountered our own version of monsoon season." He shook his head in despair. "I don't mind telling you, I really could have used the extra money those boarders would have brought in right about now. Those horses I just bought weren't exactly cheap, you know. Come to think of it, running a stable isn't exactly cheap, either."

Carole felt terrible. She knew as well as anyone how expensive it was to take care of horses. Her own horse, Starlight, used up practically all of her own allowance, as well as a healthy chunk of her father's paycheck. She couldn't even imagine how expensive it was to feed and care for more than thirty horses, as Max did. "Maybe we can talk to Mrs. Pennington," she spoke up tentatively. "If we apologize again—you know, explain that it will never happen again—"

"Forget it," Max said brusquely. "I'll deal with Mrs. Pennington myself. I don't want you three going near her. I only hope I can convince her that all my riders aren't total maniacs. She just bought a lot of the land adjoining Pine Hollow, you know. If she decides not to let my riders on her property, it will be a major inconvenience for everyone. And furthermore . . ."

"I DIDN'T THINK he would ever finish chewing us out," Carole said ruefully a few minutes later.

"I don't think he is finished," Lisa corrected. "He just had to leave to go check on the Penningtons. I'm sure he'll be back soon to yell at us some more."

Suddenly Veronica popped out of Danny's stall. She glanced around to make sure that Max was gone, then hurried toward The Saddle Club. "So, what happened?" she demanded eagerly.

"None of your beeswax," Stevie snapped. "Don't you have some important shopping or something to do? Somewhere far, far away?"

Veronica shrugged. "Fine, don't tell me. It's not like I can't guess." She prodded a limp piece of blue balloon with the toe of her expensive leather riding boots, then bent to pick it up. "You three were trying to pull some

17

sort of pathetic little prank, and it backfired." She grinned. "And just your luck—it backfired all over Mrs. Pennington and her grandson."

"Big deal," Stevie muttered. "The way Max was going on about that old woman, you'd think she was the queen of England."

Carole didn't think that was fair. Max treated all of his students and boarders with the same amount of respect— as long as they proved themselves worthy of it by taking good care of their horses.

But Veronica looked genuinely amazed at Stevie's comment. "Oh, come on!" she exclaimed. "Don't you know who the Penningtons are? They're only the most important people to move to boring old Willow Creek in years! The whole country club has been buzzing about it for weeks."

"Important?" Carole repeated in confusion.

"I think she means *socially* important," Lisa explained.

Veronica frowned. "Of course I do," she snapped. "And they are. Mrs. Pennington just bought the old Hyde mansion, and they're moving down here to Virginia from the Main Line." She smirked. "That's a very prestigious area just outside of Philadelphia, for you society outcasts."

"Big deal," Stevie said again. "If the Penningtons are so snooty, why are they bothering with little old Pine Hollow?"

Veronica rolled her eyes. "I wouldn't expect you three to know anything about society," she said, waving the piece of broken balloon airily to emphasize her point. "But I thought even you Saddle Chumps might know a little something about horse shows. When she was younger, Mrs. Pennington used to win tons of ribbons at the Devon Horse Show, and she knows Dorothy DeSoto quite well. After all, Devon is only one of the most important shows in the country."

"We know about the Devon Horse Show," Carole replied testily. She understood now why the Penningtons had come to Max about boarding their horses. Dorothy DeSoto was one of Max's former students who had gone on to have a very successful career as a competitive rider. She must have recommended Pine Hollow to Mrs. Pennington.

"Anyway," Veronica went on, "the Penningtons won't be keeping their horses here permanently. My mother said they're having the old stable on their property rebuilt. Did I mention they bought the Hyde mansion? It's probably the biggest estate in the whole county. So they just need someplace temporary while the workmen are finishing."

Just then the girls heard footsteps hurrying toward them. A second later Max appeared around the corner. His brow was furrowed, and he still looked angry. "They're still cleaning up," he reported. "Mrs. Pennington's jacket will probably have to be dry-cleaned, though she refuses to take any money for it." Suddenly he noticed Veronica standing there, smirking at The Saddle

Club. "Veronica," he said sharply, "I thought you were busy with your horse."

"Of course, Max," Veronica said sweetly. "I just came out for a second to dispose of this." She held up the piece of blue balloon, which she was still holding. "I wouldn't want Danny to choke on it."

Stevie clenched her hands in fury. That was just like Veronica—wiggling her way out of trouble while making The Saddle Club look even worse than it already did. Veronica had picked up that balloon piece in the middle of the aisle, not in Danny's stall. But there didn't seem to be much point in explaining that to Max.

"Fine." Max held out his hand, and Veronica gave him the balloon piece.

"Bye," she sang out, skipping back down the aisle toward Danny's stall and quickly disappearing inside once again.

Max returned his attention to The Saddle Club. He crossed his arms over his chest. "I don't think I've ever been more disappointed in the three of you than I am right now," he began. "I know you like to fool around"— he glared directly at Stevie at this point—"but I thought you had more sense than to endanger my horses or my business. Obviously, I misjudged you."

Carole hung her head, feeling deeply ashamed. She really had thought ahead enough to realize that they would have to pick up the balloons so that the horses wouldn't eat them. But she hadn't even considered the idea that their prank could have any other bad results—aside from making Veronica madder than ever, that is.

Lisa was feeling sheepish, too. She knew that her friends considered her the most sensible member of The Saddle Club. Why hadn't she lived up to it this time? Sure, she had made a few feeble protests about this prank. But she could have tried a lot harder to talk Stevie out of it.

Stevie felt bad about disappointing Max, too. He had yelled at her plenty of times in the past about her schemes, but this was different. Still, how could she have known that Max would be leading a stable tour right then? The last time she had seen him, he'd been alone in his office. Besides, nobody had really been hurt. If Mrs. Pennington and her grandson were such snobs that they couldn't stand a little water, maybe Pine Hollow was better off without them. After all, the last thing they all needed was a couple more country club types walking around keeping Veronica company.

"You know, I'm beginning to wonder if I've been too lenient with you girls in the past," Max went on with a deep frown. "Maybe it would be best for you to take some time off until you learn the difference between a stable and an amusement park."

Carole gasped in horror.

"But Max!" Stevie blurted out. She looked just as horrified as Carole felt. "You can't ban us from Pine Hollow. You can't!"

Max put his hands on his hips. "Oh, can't I?" he replied sourly. "Why not? Last I checked, my name is the one on the deed."

"Because we'll *die*!" Stevie spread her hands out in front of her pleadingly. "Please, Max. Punish us however you want, just not that!"

Lisa held her breath, waiting to hear what Max would say. The worst part of this whole situation was that she really couldn't blame him for wanting to revoke their riding privileges. They had acted like irresponsible little children, and that sort of behavior wasn't appropriate in a stable.

"Just give us one more chance, Max," Carole begged. Her brown eyes were wide and anxious. "We'll make it up to you. We'll muck out every stall six times a day all summer. We'll mix the grain every single week for a year. Just don't kick us out!"

Max still looked stern. "I don't know," he said. "I think maybe a couple of weeks away would—"

Suddenly Lisa remembered something. "Oh no!" she gasped, interrupting Max. "You can't ban us now. Tessa's coming tonight!"

"Tessa?" Miraculously, Max didn't look angry at being cut off in the middle of his sentence. Instead, a thoughtful expression crossed his face. "That's right. I'd forgotten she was arriving this week."

Stevie nodded. "We're picking her up right after din-

22

ner," she explained. "Just think how disappointed she'll be if she can't ride here at Pine Hollow—especially after all the wonderful things she's heard about it!"

Max shrugged. "She could still ride here," he muttered. "In fact, she could exercise your horses while you three are sitting home thinking about what you've done." But this time, his words lacked conviction.

Sensing an advantage, Lisa spoke up tentatively. "We really are sorry, Max," she said. "And it would just kill us if we thought what we did was going to ruin Tessa's visit."

"Humph." Max still looked skeptical. But then he shrugged resignedly. "Well, I suppose you didn't mean to drive me out of business. And it *would* be a shame if Tessa had to suffer for what you three did. She's a good rider, and I know she and Topside will get along splendidly." Topside was one of Max's best horses, a well-trained Thoroughbred who had once belonged to Dorothy DeSoto. The Saddle Club had already arranged for Tessa to ride him while she was visiting.

Carole crossed her fingers. She glanced down and noticed that Stevie and Lisa had already done the same. "Does that mean we're not banned?"

"All right, you're not banned," Max said. He held up a hand before the girls could speak. "Not for now, anyway. But you're on probation. One more stunt like this one and that's it. No riding for at least a month."

"That sounds fair," Carole said quickly. She took a

23

deep breath, hardly believing their narrow escape. She couldn't imagine what it would be like to be banned from Pine Hollow even for a day, let alone a whole month.

"I can only hope Tessa will be a good influence and keep you out of trouble," Max muttered. "Sweet girl. Lovely manners." Without another word, he turned and stomped off in the direction of the bathroom.

"Whew!" Stevie exclaimed as soon as he was out of earshot. "That was a close one."

Lisa saw that Stevie's face was pale. "I'll say," she agreed. "Can you imagine getting banned right before the point-to-point? I mean, I know it's not actually at Pine Hollow, but . . ."

Stevie's face got even whiter. "I didn't even think of that," she admitted. "I was too busy worrying about how to explain to Tessa why we couldn't go riding while she's here."

Danny's stall door banged open again. "Did I hear right?" Veronica demanded, looking annoyed as she came toward them again. "Is that obnoxious royal pain actually coming here for a visit?"

"If you're referring to Tessa," Lisa replied coolly, "then the answer is yes. And I'm sure she's just dying to see you, too."

"Like I care what she thinks," Veronica snapped huffily. "She may hide behind that British accent and her stupid title, but underneath it all she's just as immature and—and—*stupid* as the three of you." She whirled around and stormed back to Danny's stall.

"Uh-oh," Carole whispered. "It looks like you were right, Lisa. Veronica is holding a major grudge against Tessa. I guess she's mad that Tessa didn't recognize her superior breeding and introduce her to the queen."

Stevie rubbed her hands together. "Uh-huh," she agreed. "This could be trouble. We'll have to figure out the best way to handle it so that—"

"Stop right there, Stevie," Lisa interrupted. "In case you've already forgotten, we can't 'handle' anything right now. At least not the way you're thinking."

Carole nodded emphatically. "Lisa's right," she said. "Max is really mad this time. And the worst part is, Veronica knows it. If we do anything to her . . ." She let her voice trail off meaningfully.

Stevie nodded. She realized that her friends were right. There was no way she could risk losing her riding privileges, especially now. She would just have to wait until Max cooled off to get her revenge for "best dressed boy."

"Okay," she said. "I guess all we can do is try to keep Tessa and Veronica out of each other's way."

Carole and Lisa nodded, both looking relieved. "Right," they said in a single voice.

LATER THAT EVENING, the three friends hurried into the waiting room at the airport.

"Is her plane here yet?" Stevie asked breathlessly.

Lisa glanced up at the arrivals board, quickly scanning the listings. "There," she said. "Flight One-oh-one from London—due in at 7:45." She checked her watch. "We have ten minutes before the plane lands, and then she has to go through customs."

Carole collapsed onto one of the hard plastic chairs nearby. "I hope your dad doesn't mind waiting in the car for that long."

"He brought the newspaper, remember? Anyway, I think he really needs the peace and quiet," Lisa said. "Mom was so busy chattering at him about the point-to-point this morning that he didn't have a chance to read it over breakfast like he usually does."

Carole and Stevie laughed. Mr. Atwood had offered to wait in the car in the airport's pickup zone while The Saddle Club went inside to meet Tessa. He had claimed it was so that he wouldn't have to find a parking space. But all three girls suspected that he just wanted some time to himself. For the past few weeks, Mrs. Atwood had been so busy with the point-to-point that the Atwoods' normally quiet, sedate household had been a whirlwind of activity.

Stevie and Lisa sat down beside Carole to wait. People were rushing forward to greet the weary-looking travelers as they emerged from the customs gate.

"I think my mom was kind of disappointed about not being here to welcome Tessa to America in person," Lisa commented, tucking her legs under her chair as a portly

26

couple rushed past, chattering excitedly in a language Lisa didn't recognize. "She's pretty excited about having a real English lady staying with us. Although I think she's worried that Tessa won't think our house is fancy enough compared to what she's used to."

Stevie grinned. "She doesn't have to worry about that," she said. "Tessa probably won't even notice the difference." Despite being a distant cousin to the queen, Tessa was one of the most down-to-earth, least pretentious people the girls had ever met.

"I hope she has fun while she's here," Carole mused. She shuddered. "I still can't believe we almost ruined things by getting ourselves banned from Pine Hollow."

Normally Stevie would have teased Carole for assuming that the only way Tessa could possibly have fun during her visit was at the stable. But this time she just nodded ruefully. "I'm really sorry about that," she said. "If I'd known how that prank was going to turn out . . ."

"We know," Carole broke in. "We already forgave you after your first six thousand apologies. Besides, we should have known better, too."

Lisa nodded. "Actually, I was sort of thinking about that on the drive here," she said. "We all know that Tessa likes a good prank as much as anyone. But do you think we should maybe, um, well, avoid mentioning this particular one to her when she gets here?"

Stevie looked surprised. "What do you mean?"

Lisa wasn't sure how to explain what she was thinking

without sounding like her mother. "Well, it's just that it was kind of juvenile if you think about it—no offense, Stevie. But like Max was saying, Tessa has nice manners and everything, and she *is* a lady, even if it's easy to forget that sometimes, and we haven't seen her for a while . . ."

"I get it." Carole bit her lip. "She might not be too impressed if she heard we ended up soaking some poor, innocent bystanders and possibly ruining Max's boarding plans. It is a little immature." Her face reddened. "Besides, I'm not exactly dying to tell anyone I'm on probation with Max. I didn't even work up the courage to tell Dad about that yet."

Stevie was silent for a moment. Then she nodded. "You're right," she said briskly. "Knowing we're on probation would be a real downer for Tessa. Besides, we can't let her know that Veronica beat us this time. It makes the whole Saddle Club look bad. Tessa might not even want to be a member anymore if she found out. She might turn around and take the next plane back to England!"

Lisa thought that was a little melodramatic, even if Stevie was half joking. But she stuck out her hand. "So we keep this to ourselves," she said in a businesslike tone. "Tessa never needs to know what happened."

"Or that we're on probation," Carole added, taking Lisa's hand.

"Or that Veronica knows all about it." Stevie wrapped

28

her hand around both her friends', sealing the deal. "Mum's the word."

"There's just one problem," Carole pointed out as she pulled her hand free. "How are we going to explain to Tessa why we're *not* going to drag her over to Pine Hollow first thing tomorrow?" The three girls had already agreed to stay away from the stable the next day to give Max some time to cool off. Red had promised to look after their horses for them so that they wouldn't even have to go near the place.

"I forgot about that," Lisa admitted. "Well, we'll have to think of something. It's not like there aren't plenty of other things to see."

Carole nodded, though she didn't look entirely convinced. "We'll have to keep her out of Veronica's way," she pointed out. "Otherwise Veronica might blab and give us away."

"How hard could that be?" Stevie shrugged. "It's not as if anyone actually *wants* to spend time with Veronica di-Angelo."

"*Attention, please.*" A tinny voice came over the loud-speaker. "*Announcing the arrival of Flight One-oh-one from London, England.*"

"That's her flight!" Stevie cried excitedly. She jumped up from her seat and rushed toward the barrier separating the waiting room from customs. "Come on!"

It took some time for the passengers to disembark and

make their way through customs. But finally The Saddle Club spotted a familiar tall, slender figure heading toward them.

"There she is!" Carole squealed. "Tessa! Over here!"

All three girls waved wildly, and a second later Tessa started waving back. A wide grin lit up her face, and she rushed toward them, dragging a large suitcase behind her.

"Lisa! Carole! Stevie!" she cried, her eyes sparkling. "I can't believe I'm finally here! The flight was positively dreadful!"

"Really?" Lisa asked as the girls exchanged hugs. "That's too bad."

"Never mind," Tessa replied in her crisp British accent. "I'm exaggerating. It wasn't so bad. Well, except for the food. That was truly horrendous." She grinned at them happily.

Lisa grinned back. With all the talk her mother had been doing lately about English ladies, she was glad to see that Tessa was just the way she remembered. "I can't believe you're finally here," she said.

Stevie nodded. "I hope you got some rest on that flight. Because we've got tons of fun stuff lined up for you to do while you're here. You probably won't even have time to sleep."

"Brilliant!" Tessa replied cheerfully. "I suppose we'll be starting bright and early tomorrow morning at Pine Hollow, right?"

Lisa gulped. "Um . . ."

30

"Actually," Carole stepped in quickly, "we were thinking we'd get some of the other sights out of the way tomorrow. Not much will be happening at the stable, and we'll want to spend the whole day there on Saturday for Horse Wise."

"Right!" Lisa agreed quickly. "That's our Pony Club, by the way."

Tessa looked slightly puzzled. "I know," she said. "Your Horse Wise team came to perform in England, remember? I was there!" She grinned again. "Speaking of which, is that girl Veronica still a member? I can't wait to see her again—but only if I can help you pull more pranks on her. That business with the buried jewels was positively hysterical!"

Lisa gulped again. "Um, sure," she said. "Come on— my dad's waiting in the car. We'd better go." She led the way toward the exit, feeling worried. Maybe keeping Tessa and Veronica apart wasn't going to be as easy as they'd thought.

"I CAN'T BELIEVE IT!" Tessa exclaimed the next day through a mouthful of ice cream. "You're right, Stevie! Black cherry sauce on pistachio is positively heavenly!"

Carole and Lisa made disgusted faces as Tessa helped herself to another spoonful of Stevie's sundae. It was Friday afternoon, and all four girls were sitting in a booth at TD's, an ice cream shop near Pine Hollow. Normally Carole, Stevie, and Lisa liked to go there for Saddle Club meetings after a day of riding. Today, however, none of them had so much as set foot on Pine Hollow's grounds.

Lisa looked at her watch. "We've still got more than an hour before we have to be home for dinner. What do you want to do?" she asked.

"Well, let's see," Tessa said, setting down her spoon.

"So far today I've seen your house—of course—Stevie's house, and Carole's house." She pointed to each girl in turn as she said their names. "I've seen your schools. I've visited the country club where the point-to-point races are going to be held on the Saturday of your Independence Day weekend and the park where we're going to watch the town parade and fireworks the day after that. I've visited the mall and this shopping center, along with the Willow Creek post office and town hall. I've met all of your families, many of your neighbors, and even your headmistress, Stevie." The girls had run into Miss Fenton at the post office. "So it seems I'm just missing a couple of important items before I'll feel I've really seen everything." Tessa picked up her spoon again and reached for another bite of Stevie's sundae. "One of them is Phil, of course." Stevie had already told Tessa all about her boyfriend, Phil Marsten, who lived in a town about ten miles from Willow Creek. However, Phil was away on vacation with his family and wouldn't be back until the following week. "But aside from him, I'm simply dying to make the acquaintance of Starlight, Belle, and Prancer. Oh, and it will be lovely to see Max again, as well." Tessa popped the spoon into her mouth.

Lisa sighed. She and her friends had had a great time showing Tessa around. However, she had to admit that it had been hard to avoid the topic of Pine Hollow. "I don't think we have time for that right now," she said. "Um, I mean, not if you want to see everything."

"That's right," Carole put in. "You'll need plenty of time to really do it justice. After all, you want to meet all the horses, right? We'll have time for all that tomorrow."

Tessa looked surprised. "I can't believe my ears," she said. "Maybe I don't know you as well as I thought I did, Carole. You actually want to put off going to the stable until tomorrow?"

Carole shrugged and smiled sheepishly. "Well, I just thought it would be better to wait, since Horse Wise and our jump class are both tomorrow," she explained lamely. "We'll probably be there all day."

Tessa still looked confused, but she didn't argue. "Well, all right," she said. "Then why don't we head home and start our slumber party a bit early?"

"Cool," Stevie agreed immediately. She quickly shoveled down the last few bites of her ice cream. The others had already finished. "We'll show you what a good old American sleepover is all about."

Carole giggled. "I can sum it up in one word," she said. "Gossip!"

"Gossip about horses, I presume?" Tessa asked with a smile.

"Mostly," Lisa admitted.

"Good." Tessa stood up. "I can't wait to get started!"

"TESSA, DEAR, CAN I pour you some more tea?" Mrs. Atwood asked.

"You're too kind, Mrs. Atwood," Tessa replied politely, sliding her teacup forward across the kitchen table.

The four girls and Lisa's mother were seated around the Atwoods' large butcher-block table, where they had been since arriving from TD's more than half an hour before. For most of that time, Tessa had been sipping tea and patiently answering Mrs. Atwood's endless stream of questions about life in England.

Lisa snuck a glance at her watch. She supposed she couldn't blame her mother for wanting to talk to their guest. The night before, Mrs. Atwood hadn't returned from her committee meeting until both Tessa and Lisa were fast asleep. And that morning she had been on her way out when the girls had come down for breakfast. Still, Lisa thought, did her mother have to insist on talking about such boring stuff? Really, who cared about the rose gardens on Tessa's family estate or the latest doings of the royal family?

"Thank you so much," Tessa said as Mrs. Atwood refilled her cup.

"You're welcome, dear," Mrs. Atwood replied. She smiled and shook her head. "I just can't get over your lovely accent, Tessa. It's so—so *cultured*."

"Mom!" Lisa rolled her eyes, her cheeks turning pink. She only hoped that Tessa wasn't as embarrassed as she was. Out of the corner of her eye, Lisa glimpsed Stevie stifling a snicker.

Mrs. Atwood didn't seem to notice Lisa's consternation. "So, Tessa," she said brightly. "I'm sure the girls have told you about our little fund-raising event, haven't they? I'm so glad you'll be here for it."

"Oh, yes, the point-to-point?" Tessa said. "It sounds like jolly good fun. I love steeplechasing."

At last, Lisa thought with relief. Her mother had actually come up with an interesting topic for a change. If only she would stick with it!

Lisa decided not to take any chances. "Steeplechasing must be popular in England, isn't it, Tessa? That's where they run the Grand National and everything."

"It is rather popular," Tessa agreed. "Much more so than here in the States, from what I understand." She paused and took a sip of her tea. "But that's only natural. After all, the sport started in Great Britain."

"I've read about that," Carole said, leaning forward and looking interested for the first time since they'd arrived. "The first steeplechase took place when a couple of hunters returning home decided to race cross-country from one church steeple to another somewhere in England."

Tessa nodded. "That's right—almost. Actually, the two gentlemen were Irish. That first informal race took place in County Cork, I believe. These days, all over Great Britain, most steeplechases are a bit more formal—they're normally held at large tracks rather than out in the countryside. But the general idea hasn't changed—to get your horse from one place to another faster than your competitors without letting any obstacles stand in your way."

Mrs. Atwood looked impressed. "My, you certainly do know a lot about steeplechasing, Tessa," she commented.

Tessa shrugged. "My parents are fans of the sport," she said with a smile. "I suppose I've picked up a bit around the supper table."

"Have you ever been to the Grand National?" Carole asked.

"Just once," Tessa said. "It's run in Liverpool, which is a bit of a way from where I live. But my family watches every year on the telly."

"That's wonderful, dear," Mrs. Atwood said. "You know, I just had a marvelous idea. What would you say to being a fence judge for the junior hurdle race at our little point-to-point? It only seems right, since you know so much."

Lisa jumped in before Tessa could answer. "Mom!" she exclaimed. "That's a terrible idea! Tessa wants to *ride* in the junior hurdle—not stand around watching everyone else."

Mrs. Atwood looked taken aback, but she recovered quickly. "Oh, of course," she said. "How silly of me. Of course you'll have much more fun riding."

"Well, I was quite looking forward to it," Tessa admitted. "But thank you so much for thinking of me, Mrs. Atwood. I'm flattered that you thought I'd make a good judge."

The girl's polite comment brought the smile back to Mrs. Atwood's face. "How nice," she cooed. "Well, it's all right—we have nearly enough judges already. Even young Miles Pennington has agreed to help out. Isn't that wonderful?"

Lisa felt her face reddening at the mention of the teenage boy's name. She couldn't help picturing him as she had first seen him the day before—dripping wet. She carefully avoided meeting her friends' eyes. "That's great, Mom," she said. "So anyway, maybe it's time for us to—"

"Miles is such a lovely young man," Mrs. Atwood interrupted, still addressing Tessa. She didn't even seem to have heard her daughter. "He's one of the Pennsylvania Penningtons, you know." At Tessa's blank look, she laughed. "Oh, of course. I'm sure you wouldn't know about such things way over in England. But they're a wonderful old family. Miles's great-great-grandfather originally made his money in railroads, and . . ."

Mrs. Atwood chattered on and on about all the socially important people expected to attend the point-to-point. Lisa cast a desperate look at Stevie and Carole. She had the funniest feeling they were thinking the same thing: How could Mrs. Atwood turn an interesting topic like a full day of cross-country horse racing into such a boring conversation?

And how were they ever going to escape so that they could start the fun part of their sleepover?

4

"IT'S VERY NICE to meet you, Seattle Slew," Tessa said, bending down to scratch the head of the purring gray cat winding its way around her legs. "I'm sorry, though, we'll have to leave you behind now. We're going to visit Prancer next, and she's afraid of cats."

Lisa grinned, pleased that Tessa had remembered this detail about the Pine Hollow stable horse she usually rode. She leaned over to pat the cat. "Actually, we usually call this one Seattle Mew," she said. "Come on. Prancer's stall is right around the corner."

Tessa gave the cat one last pat, then followed. "It's so interesting that Max names all his stable cats after famous horses," she commented. "You might say it's surprisingly eccentric, actually."

Stevie raised one eyebrow and gazed at Tessa. "Oh, really?" she joked. "And this coming from someone whose family names everything in sight after characters from a bunch of musty old books?"

All four girls laughed at that, Tessa hardest of all. Her family lived on a large estate outside of London known as Dickens. The family had taken the name to heart, naming all of their horses after characters in Charles Dickens novels. For instance, during their visit the American girls had ridden horses named Copperfield, Pip, and Miss Havisham.

"Well, anyway," Tessa went on as the girls continued toward Prancer's stall, "someone should tell Max that if the people around here are serious about this point-to-point business, he really ought to name a few kittens after famous steeplechase horses."

Carole chuckled. "I guess you're right," she said. "So far we have cats named after stars in practically every other kind of horse-related sport. There are Seattle Slew, Seabiscuit, and Eclipse for flat racing; Big Ben for show jumping . . ."

"Hambletonian for harness racing," Lisa supplied.

Stevie nodded. "And don't forget Rembrandt. She's that pretty little black-and-white cat who's named after the famous dressage horse."

"Adding some steeplechase stars to the menagerie is a good idea," Lisa told Tessa. "There's just one problem—we don't really know any."

"Oh, there are plenty to choose from," Tessa insisted. "There's Lottery for one. He was the first to win the Grand National. Then you have Red Rum, Golden Miller, Desert Orchid, and all sorts of others." She grinned. "I even know of at least one rather well-known American 'chaser—Flatterer. That might be a good one to start with." She shrugged. "In fact, maybe I'll make the suggestion to Max myself when I see him. Where is he, anyway? I can't believe we've been here nearly an hour and he hasn't turned up."

"Oh, I'm sure he's around somewhere," Stevie said vaguely. She was glad they hadn't run into Max yet. She was in no hurry to come within range of his glare again.

Luckily, just then they arrived at Prancer's stall, distracting Tessa from any further thoughts about Max. "Oh, she's gorgeous!" Tessa cried in admiration.

Prancer was standing at the front of her stall with her ears perked forward curiously. She let out a snort when she saw Lisa, stretching to nuzzle her pockets for treats.

"Hi there, girl," Lisa said, giving the horse a hug. "Did you miss me yesterday? I missed you. By the way, this is our friend Tessa."

Tessa stroked the mare's nose. "Hello, Prancer," she said. "You're positively gorgeous, did you know that?"

Carole grinned. "Sure she does," she replied on the horse's behalf. "Lisa tells her all the time."

41

"I think she likes you, Tessa," Stevie remarked. Prancer had turned her attention away from Lisa and was snuffling curiously at Tessa's shoulder.

"That's no surprise, is it?" Tessa said. "You told me last night that she loves everyone under the age of twenty."

"Almost everyone," Stevie muttered, thinking of Veronica.

The four girls spent a few more minutes with Prancer, then moved on so that Tessa could meet the last few Pine Hollow residents. She also met several of the other young riders, who were starting to arrive for the Horse Wise meeting.

"The people here are all so lovely," Tessa remarked as they left yet another stall. "The horses, too. You have such a variety—frisky young things like Belle and Starlight and Romeo and Derby, chubby old darling Patch and grand old Nero, all those adorable ponies, elegant Thoroughbreds like Prancer and Calypso . . ."

Lisa nodded. She knew there were at least two Thoroughbreds at Pine Hollow that Tessa hadn't yet met. One of them was Danny, and Lisa, for one, had no intention of going near his stall. Veronica didn't usually arrive early for Horse Wise—or anything else—but there was no sense in taking chances.

"Come on," she said. "Speaking of Thoroughbreds, you still have one very important horse to meet. And we don't have much time left before we have to get to the meeting."

"Topside, right?" Tessa said eagerly. "You told me so much about him yesterday I feel as though I've met him already. I can't wait to see him in person!"

"We're sure you'll love him," Carole assured her. "Mostly because we all do—especially Stevie."

Stevie nodded. "I used to ride Topside most of the time before I got Belle," she explained. "He's fantastic. He used to belong to Dorothy DeSoto, so he's incredibly well-trained and athletic. Besides, he's the nicest, most cheerful horse you'd ever want to meet. He really loves to perform well for his rider."

Lisa grinned. "But those aren't the only reasons he's perfect for you, Tessa," she said. She winked at her friends. "You see, when we found out you were coming, we wanted to make you feel right at home."

Tessa paused in the stable aisle, looking intrigued. "What do you mean?" she asked. "Does he look like Humbug?" That was the name of Tessa's horse back home.

Carole shook her head. "Nope," she said. "But before Max's new horses arrived, we figured Topside was the closest thing we had to a real English horse."

"Now I'm truly confused," Tessa declared with a smile. "Didn't you tell me yesterday that Topside is a blue-blooded American Thoroughbred, born and raised right here in Virginia?"

"Yep," Stevie confirmed. "Topside is English by marriage, not by birth."

43

Tessa laughed out loud. "Oh, I can't wait to hear the explanation for this!"

Stevie grinned. "Like I said, he was once owned by Dorothy DeSoto . . . and Dorothy is married to Nigel Hawthorne."

Tessa gasped. "Of course! I'd forgotten about that. And Nigel is a member of the British Equestrian Team!" She clapped her hands and laughed again. "So Topside has British in-laws. I get it!" She shook her head good-naturedly. "Now I *really* can't wait to meet him. He and I will have *so* much to chat about!"

The four girls hurried to Topside's stall. After the arrival of Derby and the other newcomers, Max had moved Topside to a stall just down the aisle from Danny's. Carole gave Danny's stall an anxious glance as the girls passed, but there was no sign of Veronica. That was no real surprise. Today's Horse Wise meeting was unmounted, as every second meeting was, and it wasn't like Veronica to show up early and risk being made to do stable chores.

Tessa loved Topside just as much as her friends had expected. "Oh, he's so sweet!" she cried as the big bay gelding nuzzled her cheek. "I can't wait to ride him."

"You'll get your chance soon enough." Lisa glanced at her watch. "We have a jump class right after lunch. But now we'd better get over to the indoor ring—the Horse Wise meeting will be starting soon."

Tessa reluctantly said good-bye to Topside, then all four

girls strolled down the aisle toward the indoor ring. As they rounded the corner, they almost ran smack into Veronica.

"Watch where you're going," Veronica snapped automatically. Then she noticed Tessa behind Stevie, and her usual unpleasant frown deepened. "Oh. It's you," she said flatly, staring at the British visitor.

Tessa returned Veronica's surly comment with a sunny smile. "Hello, Veronica," she said politely. "It's marvelous to see you again. I trust you've been well?"

Veronica opened her mouth, then closed it again. "Um, sure," she muttered, shooting a suspicious glance at the other girls.

"Wonderful," Tessa said, still smiling.

Lisa couldn't help smiling, too. She was relieved that Tessa was being so polite despite Veronica's rudeness. That meant Veronica didn't have any cause for complaint, which meant Veronica had no excuse to get The Saddle Club in any more trouble with Max.

"I don't know what's so wonderful about it," Veronica said, tossing her dark hair over her shoulder and scowling at Tessa. "In fact, I think things are getting worse around here. I mean, Max is just letting anyone ride here now."

Lisa's jaw dropped in astonishment. She exchanged glances with Carole and Stevie, who also looked stunned.

Tessa wasn't thrown. She chuckled. "Oh, Veronica," she said. "You have such an interesting sense of humor!"

Veronica snorted. "Well, you have an interesting taste in friends," she said sarcastically in a bad imitation of Tessa's accent.

That was enough for Stevie. "Listen, Veronica," she said heatedly, stepping forward with her fists clenched at her sides, "that's enough. How dare you talk to our friend like—"

"Is there a problem here?" said a familiar voice.

Lisa whirled and saw Max standing in the doorway to the indoor ring with his arms folded over his chest. Mrs. Pennington was standing beside him. The old woman had a slightly bemused expression on her face. Max just looked suspicious.

Lisa gulped. "No, no problem at all, Max," she assured him hastily.

Stevie had clamped her mouth shut as soon as she realized Max was nearby. She nodded. "We're fine," she said. "We were just—uh—asking Veronica if she knew what today's meeting was about."

Veronica smirked, but she didn't say anything.

Max still looked suspicious. "Come outside and you'll find out," he said dryly. "We're meeting in the outdoor ring today." Then he saw Tessa. "Oh, hello there!" he greeted her, smiling for the first time. "Welcome to Pine Hollow."

As he introduced Tessa to Mrs. Pennington, Lisa leaned toward Carole and Stevie. "That was a close one," she murmured.

Stevie nodded and cast a glance at Veronica, who was heading outside. "She's going to be trouble," she said grimly. "I can smell it."

IT TURNED OUT that Mrs. Pennington was the guest speaker at the Horse Wise meeting. She was there to talk about her current sport, carriage driving.

"Like so many equine sports, driving began as a very practical pursuit," the elderly woman explained to the crowd of Pony Clubbers gathered around Pine Hollow's large outdoor ring. "After all, before the invention of the motor, all transportation depended on animals, especially the horse. Horses pulled fire engines, public carriages, carts that carried coal and wood and other goods, even funeral hearses. They helped with plowing and other farmwork, towed barges and trams, and carried the mail."

Carole nodded. She had read quite a bit about the hard work horses had done in the service of humankind. While she could hardly imagine a life that didn't center around horses, she knew that to many other people in the modern world, the noble animals were a novelty. But it wasn't so long ago that nearly everyone had had daily contact with working horses.

Mrs. Pennington went on to talk more about public and private coaching in the old days, as well as modern driving sports such as international driving trials, driven dressage tests, marathons, and obstacle competitions. It was very interesting, especially since so much of the information was new to most of the riders. Carole sometimes thought it was amazing that she could learn so much about horses and still find out there were all sorts of things she didn't know.

When Mrs. Pennington had finished speaking, Max stepped forward. "And now we have a very special treat," he said with a smile. "As some of you may already know, Mrs. Pennington will be boarding one of her driving teams here with us while her own stable is being renovated. They just arrived this morning, and Mrs. Pennington has graciously agreed to give us a demonstration."

"Cool!" Carole whispered.

Lisa nodded, glancing at Tessa to make sure she wasn't listening to her. "I guess this means we didn't scare her off from boarding here."

"Great!" Stevie added. "That means Max has no reason to be mad at us."

Lisa snorted. "Oh yeah?" she whispered. "Tell that to Max!"

Their conversation ceased when Miles Pennington appeared around the corner of the building. He was leading a pair of burly, glistening, perfectly matched bay horses. They were wearing a plain black leather harness, which was hitched to Max's pony cart. The cart looked even smaller than it really was behind the powerful hindquarters of the huge bays.

"I only wish my own carts and buggies had arrived in

time for this demonstration," Mrs. Pennington told the group apologetically. "But I'm afraid they aren't being shipped down from Pennsylvania for another week or so. We'll just have to make do."

Miles led the horses forward into the ring, then helped his grandmother into the cart. She picked up the reins, holding both pairs expertly in her left hand. In her right hand she held a long, slender whip, which she flicked lightly to guide her horses as they broke into a brisk trot.

"I'd like to introduce my team," the woman announced, raising her voice to be heard over the sound of the cart wheels. The horses trotted around the ring in perfect harmony. "That's Hodge on the left, and his brother Podge on the right."

Max spoke up with a smile. "Can anyone guess what breed Hodge and Podge are?"

Carole studied the two big geldings for a moment. Hodge and Podge were both a little over sixteen hands tall, solid and muscular. Each horse had a large, handsome head with a hawklike profile. They were a deep, solid bay color, with black legs, thick black manes and tails and not a speck of white to be seen on them anywhere.

Carole raised her hand.

"Yes, Carole?" Max nodded at her.

"They look like Cleveland Bays," Carole said.

Mrs. Pennington pulled her team to a stop. She glanced at Carole, looking pleased. "That's right, young lady," she confirmed. "Now I've got another question for the group. Does anyone know where the Cleveland Bay breed originated?"

Tessa raised her hand quickly. "I know!" she exclaimed. "They're British."

Veronica let out a loud snort. "Do you think *everything* comes from England?" she said sarcastically. "Come on. Everybody knows that Cleveland is in Ohio. That means Cleveland Bays must be American."

Carole did her best to keep from laughing out loud. "No, Tessa is right," she said. "The Cleveland Bay is the oldest native horse breed in Britain."

"Right," Tessa said. "Clevelands and Cleveland crosses have been kept as carriage horses in the Royal Mews in London since the nineteen twenties."

Mrs. Pennington looked impressed. "Right again," she said with a smile. "I must admit, it was a bit of a trick question." She nodded to Veronica. "So don't feel too bad, young lady. You aren't the first person I've talked to who thought my boys came from Ohio."

Lisa was used to Carole's encyclopedic knowledge of all things equine. Still, it was impressive that she knew about the Cleveland Bay breed—Tessa, too. And if Lisa was impressed, she knew that Veronica had to be positively irate. "See?" she whispered to Stevie. "We don't have to play pranks to make Veronica look bad. She does it all by herself!"

Mrs. Pennington went on. "In the old days, Cleveland Bays were generally used for farmwork or as packhorses, and they were used for hunting and coaching, as they are now. These days, when the breed is crossed with Thoroughbred blood, you can get an outstanding jumper or hunter." The woman put her team through a few more paces. Then she climbed out of the cart and answered questions from the group.

By the time the meeting came to an end, The Saddle Club had almost forgotten about Veronica's mistake about the Cleveland Bays. But Veronica clearly hadn't forgotten. As Max dismissed the group, Veronica got up and quickly hurried past the four Saddle Club girls, who were still seated on the ground. As she passed, the toe of her polished boot came down squarely on Tessa's hand.

"Ow!" Tessa cried, quickly pulling her hand away.

"Hey!" Stevie exclaimed. "Watch where you're putting your big feet!"

Veronica paused and gazed down at the other girls with a nasty smile. Then she turned her head and saw that Max was looking toward them and frowning.

"I'm *sooo* sorry, Tessa!" Veronica said loudly in a sugary voice. "I didn't see your hand there. I do hope you're okay?"

Tessa managed a small smile. "I'm fine," she said, clutching her injured hand to her chest. "It just smarts a bit, that's all. No real harm done."

"Oh, good." Veronica spun around and continued toward the stable building as Max turned to help the Penningtons with their horses.

"Did you see that?" Stevie hissed. "She did that on purpose! She only apologized because Max was looking."

"Are you all right?" Lisa leaned over to get a look at Tessa's hand.

Tessa held it out gingerly for inspection. "I'll survive," she assured her friends. "Do you really think Veronica did that intentionally?" The corners of her mouth turned up in a mischievous grin. "If so, you know what that means. This is war!"

Carole gave Lisa a worried glance. Stevie and her big mouth! If Tessa thought that Veronica had stepped on her on purpose—which of course she had—she would want to get back at her. That meant pulling pranks, and that meant The Saddle Club would be in big trouble. Maybe keeping their probation a secret from their visitor hadn't been such a good idea after all. "Come on," she said, hoping to distract Tessa from thoughts of revenge. She stood up. "Let's go inside and get some ice. That should make your hand feel better."

"Good idea," Lisa agreed, guessing what Carole was up to. "Stevie and I will join you in a second." When Carole and Tessa had disappeared inside, Lisa whirled toward Stevie. "What's the big idea?" she said. "The last thing we need right now is to start something between Tessa and Veronica. You know what Max will think about that!"

Stevie shrugged apologetically. "I know, I know," she muttered. "But Veronica is such a jerk! You know she did that on purpose because she thought Tessa was trying to make her look bad earlier."

"I know," Lisa said, "but we have to be careful."

"You're right." Stevie sighed with frustration. "But it's just as I thought. This situation with Veronica means one thing: big trouble."

Lisa couldn't help agreeing with that. "I know," she said worriedly. "Veronica knows we're on probation with Max. She knows we can't retaliate no matter what she does."

Stevie nodded grimly. "Who knows what else she'll come up with to torture us?"

"Gosh, I just love your accent, Theresa!" Simon Atherton gushed.

Stevie almost laughed out loud. She quickly took a big bite of her peanut butter and banana sandwich to stop herself. Simon, a member of Horse Wise, was one of the best-looking boys Stevie knew. He was also one of the nerdiest. He was just about the only person who called Stevie by her full name, Stephanie. And now he was doing the same thing to Tessa.

Another Horse Wise member, Betsy Cavanaugh, spoke up. "I heard you're going to be riding in the point-to-point, Tessa," she said breathlessly. "Do you go steeple-chasing all the time in England?"

Tessa and her friends had come to The Saddle Club's

favorite lunch spot, the shady hillside above the back paddock, to eat their lunches. At first it had just been the four of them, except for the mare and foal grazing on the lush summer grass below. But before long, various other members of Horse Wise had turned up to join them. Many of the young riders at Pine Hollow were curious about the British visitor, especially after hearing her smart answers in the meeting. By now there were almost a dozen people gathered on the hillside.

The American members of The Saddle Club didn't really mind. They would have plenty of time to spend alone with their friend, and they were glad that everyone except Veronica seemed to like Tessa just as much as they did. Besides, Tessa was a friendly and curious person, and she seemed to be having fun talking to her new acquaintances.

Tessa set down her empty soda can. "I've ridden in a couple of small, informal meets," she told Betsy. "I don't really know that much about it, though—just what I've picked up from my dad and mum. They're big fans."

"You know a lot more about it than we do," Meg Durham said, glancing around at her friends, who nodded in agreement. "I know there's some steeplechasing in this area, like the Maryland Hunt Cup. But a lot of us have never even seen a steeplechase in person. What's it like?"

Tessa smiled. "Oh, it's good fun!" she said. "It's really quite a lot like flat racing in some ways, though of course the jumps make things even more interesting. The horses that participate in professional steeplechasing in England are all Thoroughbreds, just like regular racehorses. I think that's true here in the States, too."

Carole nodded. "I think you're right," she said. "I know one big difference, though. Or maybe you'd call it a *small* difference." She grinned. "Steeplechase jockeys aren't as tiny as regular jockeys."

"That's true," Tessa said with a laugh, reaching over to grab a handful of Lisa's potato chips. She popped the chips into her mouth.

"Did steeplechasing really start because a couple of guys wanted to race home?" Betsy asked.

Tessa finished chewing her chips before answering. "Well, they say that's how the sport got its name." She shrugged. "But my father once told me that back in the nineteenth century, racetracks used to hold special flat races meant for working hunters only. When some people started entering their regular racehorses in the hunter races, the tracks added fences to the hunter course to keep the flat racers from running away with all the prizes. And that's how the professional sport really began."

Stevie had finished her sandwich. She leaned back on the sun-warmed grass and made herself comfortable. "Wow," she commented lazily. "Talk about a sport with history! Steeplechasing has it all: competition, intrigue, fun stories . . ."

Tessa grinned. "If you want to hear a fun story, listen to

this. Once upon a time, a group of British cavalry officers decided to have some fun. After dinner in their barracks, they put on their nightclothes—caps and shirts—over their military uniforms, saddled up their horses, and held an after-dark steeplechase race. It came to be called the Midnight Steeplechase."

Tessa's listeners laughed. "That sounds like fun!" Meg cried.

"I bet they looked awfully silly riding over fences in their pajamas," Polly Giacomin said with a grin.

Stevie was grinning, too. But her smile faded a second later when she saw Veronica coming out the back door of the stable. Veronica squinted up at their group as if trying to figure out what was going on. When she spotted Tessa, she scowled, whirled around on her boot heel, and went back inside.

Stevie glanced at Tessa. The English girl was still laughing—she hadn't even noticed Veronica's brief appearance. "Good," Stevie muttered.

"What?" Lisa asked, turning to her.

Stevie shrugged. "Nothing," she assured her. "Nothing at all."

"COME ON, WE'LL show you to the tack room," Carole said half an hour later.

It was time to get ready for jump class. The four Saddle Club girls hurried down the aisle toward the tack room.

Tessa rolled her eyes and smiled. "I already know where

the tack room is," she said. "You showed it to me at least two or three times on my tour this morning, remember? You even showed me which saddle and bridle I'm to use for Topside."

Stevie grinned. "That's Carole for you," she said. "When she gives a stable tour, she really makes it thorough."

The girls hurried into the tack room. Other members of Horse Wise were also racing in and out as they prepared for class. Some were carrying saddles and bridles. Others held grooming buckets or spare boots. Everyone seemed to be rushing. The whole scene presented a kind of controlled chaos.

The tack room itself seemed rather chaotic as well. Almost every inch of the square room was crammed with saddles, bridles, cleaning supplies, trunks, bits, stirrup leathers and irons, blankets, martingales, buckets, saddle pads, spare girths, lunge lines and cavessons, halters, and every other piece of equipment imaginable. Newcomers were often amazed that anyone could find anything they needed in the packed space, but Pine Hollow regulars knew that there was actually a very logical method to the madness. The tack room had a place for everything and everything was kept in its place—or else. Max's mother, known to one and all as Mrs. Reg, made sure of that as part of her duties of running the stable.

Carole dodged aside as Polly and Britt Lynn came rushing out with their horses' tack. "Meet you out in the aisle in two minutes," Carole called to the rest of The Saddle Club, who nodded.

She quickly moved around the room, grabbing Starlight's saddle and bridle, but paused when she heard a dismayed voice from nearby.

"Oh dear!" Simon Atherton exclaimed. "Oh dear!"

Carole stepped around Meg and Betsy, who were arguing over a pair of stirrup irons, until she could see what Simon was doing. "Oh dear is right," she said when she saw the tangled mess of leather he was holding.

Simon heard and glanced up. "Oh, hello, Carole," he said. "I seem to have gotten my reins tangled when I was taking down Patch's bridle." He shrugged and sighed. "I don't know how I do it."

Carole didn't know, either. But she offered to help him untangle the reins. With both of them working, it took only a few minutes.

"Thanks," Simon said gratefully.

Carole smiled at him and picked up her own tack again. Then she made her way through the crowd, heading for the doorway. She had nearly reached the door when Veronica came barreling in, almost crashing into her. Carole stopped short and jumped aside just in time to avoid a collision.

"Watch it!" Veronica snapped, glaring at Carole. "You could have knocked me over. And these are new breeches!"

Carole just rolled her eyes and stepped back to let the

other girl pass. Veronica was the one who had been moving too fast, but Carole knew better than to argue about it—especially now. "Sorry," she said simply.

Veronica scowled and didn't reply. As soon as she had stalked past, Carole continued on her way, emerging into the hallway once again.

Stevie and Lisa were already outside waiting for her. "Where's Tessa?" Lisa asked.

Carole shrugged. "It's a madhouse in there," she said. "I didn't even see her. Maybe she's having trouble finding Topside's stuff."

"Don't worry, she'll find it," Stevie said. "Just give her a second."

Sure enough, Tessa appeared in the doorway a moment later. But her hands were empty.

"Did you forget where Topside's tack is?" Carole asked. "Sorry, we should have showed you again."

Tessa shook her head, looking perplexed. "I remember perfectly where it was this morning," she said. "But it's not there now."

"Really?" Lisa said. "Are you sure you're looking in the right place? Our tack room can be kind of confusing."

Tessa shrugged. "I thought I had it right," she said. "But I suppose I must have gotten mixed up."

The four girls went back inside. The crowd had thinned out a bit, so it wasn't hard to make their way to the spot where Topside's bridle usually hung. The hook was empty.

Carole frowned. "Do you think someone grabbed Topside's bridle by mistake?"

"If they did, they took his saddle, too," Stevie reported. "It's not on its usual rack."

"Maybe Max or Red moved it," Lisa suggested uncertainly. "You know, the way they moved the horses around when the new ones came . . ."

"Or maybe somebody else is behind this," Stevie said grimly. She was staring across the room at Veronica, who was standing in front of an empty saddle rack with her hands on her hips and her back to The Saddle Club. "I bet Veronica moved Topside's stuff just to spite us."

Stevie started across the room, but Lisa grabbed her arm. "Stop!" she commanded. "You can't go start yelling at Veronica." Just in time, she remembered that Tessa still didn't know their secret. "Um—it's not nice," she finished lamely.

"Are you *daft*?" Tessa said. "Lisa, if Veronica took my tack, there's just one thing to—"

Before she could finish her sentence, a loud wail came from across the room. "Hey!" Veronica cried. "Who took Danny's saddle?"

Carole's jaw dropped. "Huh?" she said to her friends.

Stevie hoisted her own saddle to her other arm and shook her head. "Huh," she grunted.

At that moment Red O'Malley entered. "Five minutes, everyone," he called. "Max is almost ready to get started in the outdoor ring."

"Red!" Veronica called. "I have a problem. My tack is missing. Someone stole it!" She spun around and surveyed the few people left in the tack room. Seeing The Saddle Club, she frowned and pointed at them. "I bet they took it to make me look bad! That's just the kind of stupid little joke they're always playing around here."

Beside her, Carole heard Stevie gasp. "Why, that rotten, stinking . . . ," Stevie muttered.

Before Carole could say anything, Tessa stepped forward. "I'm afraid you're wrong about that, Veronica," she said calmly. "You see, my tack seems to be missing as well."

Red looked confused. After shooing the other remaining members of the jump class out the door, he turned back to Veronica and The Saddle Club. "Okay, let me get this straight. We have two missing saddles?"

"And bridles," Tessa supplied helpfully. "At least mine is missing."

"Mine too," Veronica put in quickly. She tossed her head. "And if it doesn't turn up soon, there's going to be trouble."

Carole thought there was trouble brewing already, but she didn't say so. "Come on," she said. "Someone may have moved the stuff by accident. Let's take a look around."

"Good idea, Carole," Red said, still looking a little confused. "Let's split up and search."

Just then, Britt came back into the tack room. "Oh,

there you are, Red," she said softly. "Um, I was just giving Magoo's stall a quick cleaning, and when I went out to the muck heap I saw something weird. There are a couple of saddles lying out there."

"Do you think Red believes we didn't do it?" Lisa whispered to Stevie a short while later. The jump class was in full swing. At the moment, Max was watching as Carole, Tessa, Veronica, and a couple of other students jumped all together over a series of wide obstacles. Most of the horses were used to jumping solo, and Max wanted them to be comfortable jumping in a group before the point-to-point. Stevie and Lisa were waiting for their turns.

Stevie didn't answer for a second. She was watching Veronica, who was doggedly urging Danny forward as Topside pulled ahead a few strides. Even though this wasn't meant to be a race, it was clear that Veronica didn't want to let Tessa get ahead of her even for one second.

Stevie glanced at Lisa and frowned. "The real question is, do you think he believes Veronica *did* do it?" she whispered back.

Thanks to Britt, Veronica and Tessa had found their saddles and bridles in the muck heap. They were a bit dirty and smelly but otherwise all right. Veronica had once again accused The Saddle Club of playing a prank. The Saddle Club had pleaded innocent, but a spark of doubt had remained in Red's eyes. He hadn't mentioned their probation, but it was obvious—to the American members, anyway—that he knew about it.

Lisa sighed. "I guess we're just lucky Red agreed not to tell Max."

"True," Stevie said ruefully. "And we're lucky we were all so busy getting Tessa's tack cleaned up that she didn't have time to ask any awkward questions."

"I know." Lisa nodded. "Do you think we're doing the right thing by keeping all this a secret?"

Stevie hesitated. She had thought they were doing the right thing in the beginning, but lately she had started to wonder. Maybe it would be better to tell Tessa about their probation. Then she would understand why they couldn't get into any fights with Veronica.

She opened her mouth to say so. But at that moment, Max turned and glared at her. "No talking in class!" he barked. "Lisa, you and Prancer are up in the next group. Move it!"

As the jump class ended, Max called to Lisa. "Could you wait a moment?" he said. "I need to talk to you."

Lisa nodded and led Prancer toward him, feeling nervous. What did Max want to talk to her about? Had Veronica told him about the tack incident? Even though Red had promised to keep quiet, Lisa wouldn't put it past Veronica to tattle to Max herself.

But it turned out to have nothing to do with Veronica.

"I wanted to speak to you about the point-to-point," Max said. He reached out and patted Prancer on the neck. "I should have brought it up earlier, but I must admit I've been so busy lately that it didn't occur to me until now. You'll need to choose another horse to ride in the junior hurdle race, and you really ought to start practicing on that horse from now until the event."

"Another horse?" Lisa repeated blankly. Then she gasped. "Oh no!" she exclaimed. "You mean you don't think Prancer should run in that kind of race, either?"

Prancer had been a racehorse before coming to Pine Hollow. Her career at the track had ended because of an inherited weakness in her leg that showed up when she ran at top speed. Now Lisa realized that Prancer's weak leg was likely to cause problems in a jumping race as well.

Max noticed her consternation and gave her a sympathetic look. "I'm sorry, Lisa," he said gently. "I know you and Prancer are a fine pair. But this sort of thing just isn't safe for her."

"I know," Lisa said, swallowing hard. "You're right. I should have thought of that myself." *Normally I would have*, she told herself. But between planning for Tessa's visit, helping her mother plan for the event, and fighting with Veronica, she hadn't had time to think about much else.

Her mind was still spinning with the bad news as she

finished grooming Prancer and headed for the tack room to meet her friends. All three of them were already there, cleaning their saddles and bridles.

Carole looked up as she came in. "Hi, Lisa," she said. Her forehead crinkled. "Hey, what's wrong? What did Max want?"

Lisa dropped Prancer's saddle onto a rack and collapsed on a handy trunk. "Bad news," she reported. She quickly filled them in on the problem. "So now I've got to figure out which horse I want to ride in the race," she finished heavily. "Max said the choice is up to me."

"Oh dear," Tessa said sympathetically. "That's too bad." She grinned weakly. "But I suppose it's good news for me. Now, with the real racehorse out, Topside and I are certain to win!"

Veronica walked in just in time to hear Tessa's comment. She stared at the girl with a frown. "You're awfully confident for someone who's never even seen a real American point-to-point," she snapped. She dropped Danny's sweaty tack on a rack. "But your title and accent aren't going to help you out on the course. I can promise you that!" She turned and stomped out of the room without another glance at her dirty tack.

Lisa frowned. It was just like Veronica to leave her work for someone else to do—and equally like her to jump to the worst possible conclusion about a member of The Saddle Club. Lisa knew that Tessa's remark had been a joke intended to cheer her up. But Veronica had obviously taken it as a serious boast.

"What a piece of work she is!" Tessa exclaimed, staring after Veronica.

Stevie nodded grimly. "That's the understatement of the year."

"THIS IS LOVELY," Tessa said quietly, signaling for Topside to stop beside Starlight. She gazed around in awe. Dappled sunlight poured through the leafy tree branches rising overhead and bounced off the surface of the creek as it gurgled between mossy, rock-studded banks.

Lisa smiled as she watched Tessa's reaction to The Saddle Club's favorite spot. It was the following afternoon, and the four friends were taking a leisurely trail ride. "Do you like it?" she asked.

"I don't just like it," Tessa declared. She smiled. "I *love* it!"

"That proves it, then," Stevie said. "You really were meant to be a member of The Saddle Club!"

"Was there any doubt?" Tessa asked, pretending to look hurt.

"Not for a moment," Carole assured her, swinging down out of the saddle.

When the girls had tied their horses in the shade of some nearby trees, they walked down to the bank and removed their boots. Soon all four of them were dangling their toes in the cool, rushing water.

"That feels good," Tessa said. "My legs are still aching from that jump class yesterday."

Carole grinned. "Are you sure that's what did it?" she teased. "You were doing a lot of jumping up and down and cheering at that baseball game last night."

"Hey," Tessa joked back. "I was just trying to fit in and enjoy the American national pastime!"

The evening before, the four girls had decided to show Tessa a bit of Americana by taking her to Stevie's older brother Chad's intramural baseball game. Tessa and her hosts had had a wonderful time eating popcorn, shouting encouragement at the players, and even lifting Chad onto their shoulders at the end of the game to celebrate his winning run.

"That was fun," Lisa said happily. "But I'm with Tessa. Max really worked us hard yesterday—even my toes are sore." She wiggled them in the creek to emphasize her point.

"He did work us hard," Carole agreed. "But I'm glad he

did. I want to be ready for the junior hurdle race. It's not like anything we've ever done before."

"I can't believe the point-to-point is less than two weeks away," Stevie said.

"Speaking of which," Lisa said, brushing a stray twig off her leg, "we still haven't talked much about my problem. I don't have a horse to ride in the junior hurdle."

"Well, it's not as if Max said *you* couldn't enter the race," Stevie pointed out. "You just can't ride Prancer. You'll have to pick another school horse."

"I know." Lisa hated the thought of riding a different horse in the exciting event, but the logical side of her knew it was for the best. She didn't want Prancer to reinjure her leg any more than Max did. "The trouble is finding a good one that isn't already being ridden by somebody else."

"Well, let's think about this," Carole said, sounding almost as logical as Lisa. "Who do we have entered in the junior hurdle so far? Stevie and I are riding our own horses, of course. So are Veronica and Polly and Britt and Andrea."

Stevie nodded and ticked off more names on her fingers. "Betsy Cavanaugh will be riding Barq, as usual. Joe Novick will be on Rusty. Meg Durham, Diablo. Meg Roberts, Comanche."

Lisa continued the list. "Lorraine Olsen, Coconut," she said. "Helen Sanderson, Eve. Simon Atherton, Patch. Anna McWhirter, Bluegrass. Adam Levine, Tecumseh."

"Even the younger riders are using up some of the good horses," Carole pointed out. "They don't all ride ponies. Melanie has been riding Chip lately in Horse Wise, and Peter Allman is crazy about Harry."

"Oh dear," Tessa said. "Now I'm feeling awful about using up Topside. Who normally rides him?"

"Adam does sometimes," Carole explained. "But Max usually rides him during our lessons and stuff."

"Don't worry about it," Lisa told Tessa. "I'm happy you'll be riding Topside." She forced herself to smile. "He's an almost English horse for our English rider, remember? I only wish there was another horse for me." She sighed ruefully. "Just about the only ones left are Calypso and Nero." Calypso, a beautiful Thoroughbred mare, had recently foaled and was in no shape for competition. But she still could have beaten Nero, the oldest horse at Pine Hollow, who rarely moved faster than a stately walk.

Carole shook her head. "Wow. I guess now we know why Max bought those new horses. Pine Hollow is getting so popular that—"

"That's it!" Stevie cried.

"Huh?" Carole asked.

"Don't you see?" Stevie explained impatiently. "It's so obvious. Lisa will have to ride one of the new horses! Isn't that exciting?"

Lisa looked a little uncertain. "I don't know," she said. "They just got here. Nobody in our class has even tried any of them out yet."

71

Stevie shrugged. "So what?" she said. "Max and Red have been riding them a lot to make sure they're ready. They look great. Especially Derby—he's got some fantastic moves. I saw Red schooling him over some jumps just the other day."

"Derby?" Tessa said. "What a cute name! It makes him sound very English."

"He *is* English," Carole told her. "Max bought all three of the new horses from a dealer he knows in Newmarket."

"Really? Some of the best trainers and breeders in England live there," Tessa said. "You really must try him, Lisa! Then you can help me properly represent Great Britain in this point-to-point." She winked. "In a way, I suppose all the horses here are *English* horses—that is, you ride them English-style instead of Western—but you'll be the only one riding a *truly* English horse. I'm rather jealous!"

Lisa laughed. "Well, when you put it that way, how can I say no?" she quipped. She took a deep breath. "All right, I'll talk to Max about giving Derby a try."

"Brilliant!" Tessa cried. She started whistling "God Save the Queen" as the four girls stood and made their way to their horses for the ride back.

Once they were in the saddle, they continued to chat about Derby and the other new horses for a few minutes. Then, gradually, all four girls fell silent, just enjoying the ride and the beautiful summer day.

Stevie was the first to notice the sounds. "Hey, what's

that?" she said, cocking her head to one side to listen better. "It sounds like hammering."

The others listened, too. "It's definitely hammering," Lisa said slowly. Suddenly her eyes lit up. "Oh, I know. I think we're riding on the Penningtons' land right now. That must be the construction crew working on their stable."

"Of course," Carole said immediately, and Stevie and Tessa nodded.

"Mrs. Pennington's talk at the meeting yesterday was so interesting, wasn't it?" Tessa commented. "She really knows a lot about driving. And her Cleveland Bays are gorgeous! I'd love to talk with her some more sometime, wouldn't you?"

"Uh, yeah," Stevie lied. She planned to stay as far away from both Penningtons as possible for the time being. Maybe someday Mrs. Pennington and her grandson would forget about that water balloon incident. But until they did . . .

"So!" Carole said, a little too brightly. "What do you say we do a little practicing for the point-to-point when we get back? The horses aren't very tired, and I'm sure you could give us some tips, Tessa."

"Sure, I'll do what I can," Tessa said agreeably.

As the English girl started chatting about steeplechasing, Stevie let out a small, hidden sigh. She was beginning to wonder why she and Carole and Lisa had ever wanted to keep their probation a secret from their friend.

The secret was starting to become more of a problem than the problem itself.

"OH, CAROLE, THERE you are," Meg Durham called, hurrying into the tack room. "Can you give me a hand for a second? Max asked me to clean out that little nick on Diablo's fetlock, and he won't stand still even in the cross-ties."

Carole glanced up. The Saddle Club had just finished their practice, and Carole was helping Tessa reattach the noseband on Topside's bridle after its cleaning. It was a new one, and the leather was a little stiff. "No problem, Meg," she said as the noseband snapped into place. "I'll be right there." She started to stand up.

But Meg was frowning. "Oh, um, never mind," she said quickly, giving Tessa a strange look. "I didn't realize you were busy. I can, um, get Red to help me."

Carole shrugged. "Suit yourself," she said, although Meg had already left the room.

"She seemed in an odd mood," Tessa commented, standing to hang the bridle back on its hook.

Carole just shrugged again, not very interested in Meg's mood. Meg was usually nice, but she was also friendly with Veronica, and that meant that nothing she did surprised Carole very much. "Come on," she said. "Let's go see if Stevie and Lisa are finished mucking out those stalls."

They left the tack room and wandered down the aisle, looking for their friends. They didn't find them with Belle or Prancer, so they continued along the stable aisle, checking each stall. As they walked past the stall that housed Barq, a popular Pine Hollow school horse, Betsy Cavanaugh popped her head out over the half door.

"Oh!" she said, seeming startled to see them. She stared fixedly at Tessa, her mouth hanging slightly open.

"Hi, Betsy," Carole said. "Have you seen Stevie or Lisa lately?"

Betsy didn't answer. She was still gazing at Tessa.

"Betsy?" Carole repeated.

"Um, what?" Betsy said. "Oh, by the way, did you hear the news? Barq is probably just about ready to retire."

"What?" Carole furrowed her brow, confused. "Barq ready to retire? What are you talking about?" She glanced at Barq, who had come to the front of his stall to see what was going on. Carole knew that the spirited Arabian gelding was only about nine years old, fairly young for a riding horse.

Betsy didn't answer. Instead she ducked back inside the stall, shoving Barq away from the door.

"What was that all about?" Tessa asked.

Carole shook her head. She had no idea. Like Meg, Betsy was friendly with Veronica. "I don't know, and I don't want to know," she said, making a mental note to check with Red to make sure Barq was okay.

75

The two girls continued down the aisle. They finally found Stevie and Lisa mucking out Derby's stall.

"Getting acquainted with your new pal?" Carole asked Lisa.

Lisa smiled. "Don't tell Prancer I said so, but I think this might work out after all. Derby seems like a real sweetheart."

"And Max said she can try him out tomorrow," Stevie added, looking up from sweeping the area in front of the stall.

Carole grabbed a pitchfork that was leaning against the wall. She glanced up at the tall chestnut, who was calmly watching the girls work. "Don't worry, boy," she told him with a smile. "We'll have your stall all fresh and tidy in no time."

Tessa stepped forward to pat Derby on the neck. "I say, he really is quite the looker, isn't he?"

A loud snort came from the aisle. "Yeah, I bet," muttered a voice.

Carole turned and saw Joe Novick, a boy from Horse Wise. "Oh, hi, Joe," she said. She noticed that the normally good-looking boy had an ugly scowl on his face. He was staring from Tessa to Derby and back again. "What's wrong?"

"You'll find out soon enough," he muttered. "We all will." With that, he turned and hurried off down the aisle before the astonished girls could say another word.

"What's gotten into him?" Lisa wondered, leaning on the shovel she'd been using and staring after Joe.

"I don't know," Carole said slowly. "But whatever it is, it seems to be contagious." She quickly told Lisa and Stevie about Meg's weird behavior in the tack room and Betsy's even stranger remarks about Barq.

Tessa's forehead wrinkled in consternation. "You know, if I were a paranoid person, I would start to worry," she said. "All those kids seemed to be giving me the evil eye."

"Hmmm," Stevie said. She stepped into the middle of the aisle and glanced around. "I'm getting a funny feeling about this. I think it's about time we got to the bottom of it."

One of the younger riders, a seven-year-old boy named Liam, was walking toward them as he headed for his pony's stall. Stevie strode over and grabbed his arm. "Hey, Liam," she said in a friendly tone. "Come here a second. We want to ask you something."

Liam glanced up at her, then shot a suspicious look at Tessa. "What do you want?" he asked Stevie, his lower lip jutting forward slightly in a defiant pout.

Tessa stepped forward. "Hello, Liam," she said. "Remember me? I was at your Horse Wise meeting yesterday."

Liam shrugged and stared down at the ground, looking uncomfortable. He didn't say anything.

Carole frowned. Liam was normally a friendly, polite

boy. What was going on here? "What's wrong with everyone today?" she blurted in exasperation. "Liam, why are you being so rude to Tessa?"

Liam looked up and glared at Carole stubbornly. "I don't want her to take Nickel away," he muttered.

For a second Carole wasn't sure she'd heard him correctly. "What?" she said. "What are you talking about, Liam? Why would you think—"

"Veronica," Stevie interrupted grimly. She bent down until she was eye level with the little boy. "Did Veronica diAngelo tell you Tessa wanted to take your pony away?"

"No." Liam shrugged. "It was some of the other kids. Jackie and Corey were talking. They said she"—he indicated Tessa with a nod of his head—"came here from England to buy all the good horses and ponies at Pine Hollow. She wants to send them back to England for the queen to ride."

Carole was speechless. So Stevie was right! No matter who had told Liam the rumor, there was no doubt about who had started it. If Veronica had one true talent, it was spreading malicious gossip.

Luckily Lisa's voice hadn't deserted her. She bent down beside Stevie and gazed earnestly at the little boy. "Listen, Liam," she said gently. "Jackie and Corey are wrong. Tessa's here visiting me and my friends. She's not going to take any of our horses back to England with her."

Liam still looked suspicious. "Really?" he asked, shooting a glance at Tessa.

Tessa nodded emphatically. "Really, truly," she said. "Cross my heart and hope to die. I'm not after your pony. I promise."

Liam looked relieved. "That's great!" he exclaimed. "I really like riding Nickel. And he wouldn't like it much in England." With that, he skipped off down the aisle.

Stevie shook her head and picked up her broom again. "Can you believe the nerve of that girl?" she muttered.

"Stevie . . . ," Carole said warningly. She didn't want Stevie getting Tessa riled up about Veronica.

But when she glanced at the British girl, she saw that it was too late. Tessa's eyes were practically shooting sparks. "I've had just about enough of this!" she exclaimed.

"Don't worry about it," Lisa said quickly. "Um, it's not worth it."

"She's right," Stevie said. "Uh, Veronica's a jerk to everyone. The best thing is just to ignore her."

Carole was sure that last remark had pained Stevie a lot. "That's the best thing," she added. "Just ignore her and forget about it. That's what we always do. Right, guys?"

"Right!" Stevie and Lisa chorused, sounding almost convincing.

Tessa shook her head sadly. "But how can I forget this?" she said. "Everyone at Pine Hollow thinks I'm the next best thing to a horse thief. No wonder everyone is giving me dirty looks! Don't you think this requires a little creative retaliation?"

79

Carole avoided meeting her eye as she shook her head. "It's not worth it," she said. "Really. It only encourages her."

Tessa was silent for a long moment. "Well, okay," she said at last, biting her lip. "If you say so." She sighed. "But I've at least got to talk to some of the people she told—you know, clear my good name. I'll be back soon, okay? I'm going to see if Betsy and Joe and Meg are still around."

The other girls didn't try to stop her. When Tessa was out of earshot, Carole sighed loudly. "Wow," she said, attacking the dirty straw in Derby's stall with new energy. "What are we going to do now?"

"I think we headed her off this time," Lisa said. "But you know there's going to be a next time . . . and a next time . . ."

"I know," Stevie said. "I think it's about time we just—"

"Well, hello," a snide voice interrupted her. "Where's your little foreign friend?"

"Hello, Veronica," Stevie replied icily. "What are you doing here? Is the mall closed?"

Veronica didn't reply. She just leaned back against the wall outside Derby's door, looking smug and self-satisfied. "I do hope *Lady* Theresa is enjoying her little visit to America," she purred.

Carole glanced anxiously at Stevie. Veronica was obviously trying to goad them.

But she needn't have worried. Stevie was smiling calmly. "You know, Veronica, you really should talk to Mr. French sometime."

Veronica looked confused but wary. "Mr. French?" she repeated. "Why on earth would I want to talk to him?" Mr. French was one of Max's adult riders.

"Well, he works for the State Department, so he might be able to give you some career advice," Stevie explained. "Because with your personality, you're definitely destined for a career as a diplomat."

Veronica's eyes narrowed. "Very funny, Stevie," she said sarcastically.

"Uh-huh," Stevie went on as if she hadn't heard her. "If we—I mean you—are really lucky, maybe you'll get sent someplace really great. Like Timbuktu."

She burst out laughing at her own joke. Carole and Lisa did the same, feeling relieved. Their riding privileges were safe—for a little while longer, at least.

And all Veronica could do was stand there and glare at them.

THE NEXT MORNING when Lisa arrived downstairs for breakfast, she found Tessa there ahead of her. The visitor was sitting at the kitchen table with Mrs. Atwood. Papers were spread out across the table, covering every bit of the surface except for the small space occupied by Tessa's cereal bowl.

"Morning." Lisa greeted her mother and Tessa with a yawn. "What are you guys doing?" She grabbed a clean glass out of the cabinet and sat down beside Tessa.

Mrs. Atwood smiled eagerly. "Oh, Tessa and I were just looking over the course plans for the point-to-point races," she said. "The course designer we hired finished them yesterday, and since Tessa knows so much about these things, I thought—"

"What?" Lisa broke in, aghast. She quickly glanced at the large sheet of paper spread in front of Tessa. "Mom, you're not supposed to show her those! She's riding in the race, remember? None of us are supposed to see the course until the morning of the event!"

"Oh, Lisa," Mrs. Atwood began with a little laugh. "Tessa said something about that too, but I'm sure no one would mind if—"

"Mom!" Lisa exclaimed. Now she knew exactly what was going on. Obviously, Mrs. Atwood had wanted to show Tessa the course map. Tessa had politely demurred. Mrs. Atwood had ignored her protests and insisted on showing her anyway, and Tessa had been too polite to refuse. Lisa quickly grabbed the map and flipped it facedown on the table. "You don't understand," she told her mother in exasperation. "People take this stuff seriously. It's not fair if one person has an advantage. You shouldn't have made her look."

"It's all right, Lisa," Tessa put in quickly. "I didn't see that much. And I promise to block what I saw out of my mind before the race." She crossed her heart and smiled tentatively.

Lisa could tell the other girl felt a little uncomfortable, so she decided to let it drop. "I know you will, Tessa," she said.

"I'm sorry, Lisa," Mrs. Atwood said, looking upset. "I didn't realize it was such a problem to let Tessa look over the plans." She grabbed the map and quickly rolled it up.

"It's just that there's so much to do, and I really don't understand a lot of the details of this sort of thing, and—"

"It's all right, Mom," Lisa said, feeling a little guilty. She grabbed the pitcher from the counter and poured herself some orange juice. "It's no big deal, really. Nobody ever needs to know."

"Well . . ." Mrs. Atwood still looked uncertain.

"Really, Mrs. Atwood," Tessa said graciously. "You couldn't possibly have known. It will be all right."

". . . AND TESSA TRIED to explain that, but Mom just bull-dozed ahead and showed her anyway. Can you believe it?" Lisa said.

She was in the student locker room at Pine Hollow with Tessa, Stevie, and Carole. She and Tessa had just finished telling the others about what had happened at the breakfast table.

Carole smiled. "It sounds like your mom was just being her usual self," she said, tossing her sneakers into her cubbyhole and reaching for her riding boots. "But I'm sure she didn't mean any harm by it."

"Of course not," Tessa agreed. "And there's no harm done." She grinned and lowered her voice to a whisper. "I didn't want to say it in front of your mum, Lisa, but I didn't see much of anything on that map, anyhow. As soon as she opened it up, I crossed my eyes so that I wouldn't be able to. Like this, see?" She crossed her eyes and made a silly face.

Her friends burst out laughing. "Do you do that when you have tea with the queen?" Stevie joked.

Before Tessa could respond, Veronica entered. She gave them all a sour look. "Is this what you do at your little club meetings?" she asked snippily. "Sit around and make faces at each other?"

Stevie gritted her teeth. She was really getting tired of having to roll over and take Veronica's obnoxious comments all the time. She wouldn't have been able to stand it at all if her riding privileges hadn't been on the line. "Come on, guys," she said to her friends. "Let's get out of here. We should get to work." The four friends had planned to do some more practicing for the point-to-point.

Veronica snorted. "Oh, but why bother?" She smirked nastily at Tessa. "I thought you and Topside had the junior hurdle all sewn up. Or did you finally realize that we Americans know how to ride, too?"

"That's enough!" Tessa cried.

Carole knew they couldn't let Tessa get into a shouting match with Veronica and opened her mouth to say something, but Lisa was clearly thinking the same thing. "Tessa," Lisa began, placing a soothing hand on her arm.

But Tessa shook it off. She was still glaring at Veronica with her fists clenched at her sides. "I've had just about enough of your little comments!" she said. "I've tried to be polite, but—"

"Tessa!" Stevie broke in desperately. "Come on. Don't stoop to her level."

"That's right," Carole agreed. "We don't have time. We're supposed to be practicing now, remember?"

Their comments obviously surprised Tessa enough to silence her. She turned and gave them a perplexed look. "But she's done nothing but insult me since I got here," she protested. "I can't let her get away with that, can I?"

"Oh, please," Veronica said. She gave a loud yawn. "I'm bored by this conversation. Now I understand why everyone says British people are dull." She stalked out of the room.

Tessa scowled and started after her, but her friends held her back.

"Forget about her," Carole advised, feeling guilty. What kind of friends were they being to Tessa, anyway? First they decided to keep an important secret from her—that decision had made sense at the time, though Carole couldn't imagine why—and now they were letting Veronica stomp all over her. She knew that Tessa would understand if they told her why they couldn't get back at Veronica. Maybe it was time to spill their secret. Still, she didn't want to say anything until she talked it over with Stevie and Lisa privately. The whole Saddle Club had to be in agreement.

"Come on," Lisa said, heading for the door. "Let's go get our tack."

Tessa sighed and nodded. "All right," she said glumly. "Lead the way."

LISA WAS HAPPY to see that Tessa's mood had improved by the end of their practice. Lisa was feeling pretty good, too. She was riding Derby for the first time, and the big gelding was just as wonderful as she had hoped. He had smooth, even paces and seemed eager to please his rider. She still missed Prancer, of course, but she was sure that she and Derby would be able to do well in the point-to-point race. And even more important, Prancer's leg wouldn't be put at risk.

The girls spent more than an hour in an unoccupied pasture practicing skills they would need for the competition. At the end of the session, they even held a mock race over some low obstacles, with a candy bar from the Pine Hollow vending machine standing in for a blue ribbon.

Lisa decided not to push Derby to win this time. It was more important to make sure the two of them could work well as a team first. She was happy to find that the big chestnut seemed eager to race, but she was even happier that he obeyed her signals to take it easy. He jumped each fence a few strides behind the others, who were battling for the win. Tessa and Topside were in the lead for most of the way, with Carole and Starlight a close second. But at the last fence, Belle surged forward with a new burst of energy, carrying Stevie to victory.

"Yahoo!" Stevie cried, pumping her fist in the air as she crossed the finish line they had marked in the grass. "We did it!" She circled back to rejoin her friends. "And that was just a warm-up. I can't wait until I beat everyone in the real race." She grinned. "Especially Phil."

Lisa rolled her eyes, but then she smiled. She could tell that Stevie was just joking—this time. Stevie and her boyfriend were both very competitive people, which had caused problems between them in the past. But lately both Stevie and Phil had learned to take things a lot less seriously. They still loved to compete and win, but they didn't let it come between them.

Tessa leaned forward to pat Topside. "Well, don't get too cocky, Stevie," she said cheerfully. "I'm sure Topside here was just holding back a bit—you know, conserving his energy for the real race. We may surprise you yet."

"Yeah, yeah." Stevie waved one hand airily. "That's what they all say!"

All four girls laughed. Then they dismounted and started cooling down their horses, who were sweaty and tired after all the exercise.

"Speaking of Phil," Tessa said as they walked around the corner of the stable building, "I can't wait to meet him. When does he return from his holiday?"

"Tomorrow," Stevie said. "And he definitely wants to meet you, too. I'll call him tomorrow and see if we can figure out a plan for later this week."

Tessa nodded and opened her mouth to answer, but just then Anna McWhirter came hurrying out the side door. She stopped short when she spotted The Saddle Club.

"Hi," Lisa greeted her.

Tessa smiled. "Hello, Anna," she said at the same time.

Anna scowled. "Hi," she said shortly. Then she spun around and raced back the way she had come.

"Uh-oh," Stevie said. "That was weird. Are you thinking what I'm thinking?"

Tessa looked worried. "Do you think she still believes that silly rumor about me buying all your horses? I thought I convinced her it was nonsense."

Carole shook her head. "Anna's no fool," she said. "She wouldn't believe something like that." *But who knows what else Veronica might be telling people?* she added silently.

"Let's keep moving," Lisa put in. "We've got to get these guys cooled down."

By the time Carole, Stevie, and Lisa met up in the tack room a little later, they all knew something was going on.

"Adam Levine walked by while I was grooming Starlight," Carole reported, glancing over her shoulder in case Tessa walked in. The British girl was still busy in Topside's stall, and the others didn't want her to hear them. "He made some kind of weird comment about how I should watch my back."

Stevie nodded grimly. "Betsy Cavanaugh said something like that to me, too," she said. "When I asked her what she meant, she wouldn't tell me. Her face got all red and she kept playing with her hair. Then she ran away."

Lisa sighed. "It's obvious that Veronica is spreading rumors again," she said. "We'd better find out exactly what she—"

"Hi, Tessa!" Carole interrupted brightly. "Is Topside all bedded down and comfy?"

Tessa nodded. "He's fine," she said shortly, dropping Topside's saddle onto an empty rack. "Listen, you guys, I think something is up. That little girl from Horse Wise—I think she's called Jessica—passed me in the hall while I was refilling Topside's water bucket. She took one look at me and burst into tears. Then she ran away."

Carole gulped. This was bad. "Um, we think maybe there's another rumor going around about you," she said carefully. "Now, we can't prove Veronica is behind it, but—"

"Of course she is," Stevie snapped. Then she seemed to remember the situation. "Uh, I mean, I guess you're right. You never know. Innocent until proven guilty—that's the American way, right?"

Tessa looked ready to protest, but Lisa jumped in before she could say anything. "The best thing to do is probably just ignore it," she suggested. "Come on, let's finish up with this tack, and then we can head over to TD's."

"But—" Tessa began.

"So, did Derby have any problems with those fences, Lisa?" Carole said brightly, cutting her off. "He looked pretty good out there."

"Oh, he was," Lisa said. She shot a glance at Tessa's confused face, feeling terrible. She knew Tessa was unhappy about what was going on, and she couldn't blame her. Still, what could they do? Later, she would have to find a way to talk to Carole and Stevie alone. Maybe they would agree to tell Tessa about the probation. That would make things a lot easier for all of them. "He really seems to love jumping."

Just then Polly stuck her head into the tack room. "Oh, excuse me," she said with a frown, staring at Tessa. "I didn't know anyone was in here." She started to leave, then hesitated. "You know, I wasn't going to say anything," she said, "but some people around here should realize they're not as great as they think they are." She spun and left, almost bumping into Simon Atherton, who was just entering.

"Okay, that's just about enough!" Tessa cried. "I want to know what's going on around here! Suddenly I feel like some kind of leper!"

"Hey, Simon," Lisa said, scrubbing angrily at a spot on Derby's saddle. "Do you know why Polly's so upset?"

Simon shrugged, looking nervous. He shot a glance at Tessa. "Um, why, n-no," he stammered. "I have no idea."

"Come on," Carole urged. "What's going on around here? You can tell us. Please, Simon?" Simon still hesitated, so Carole grabbed the candy bar that was sticking out of Stevie's shirt pocket.

"Hey!" Stevie protested. "I won that fair and square!"

Carole ignored her. "Here," she said, handing the candy bar to Simon. "Call it a bribe if you want. But we really need to know the truth."

Simon hesitantly took the candy bar. He stared at it for a moment, then gulped. "Well, I really shouldn't say anything . . ."

Tessa jumped up from her seat on an overturned bucket and hurried over to him. "Please, Simon," she begged. "I need your help. Everyone seems to hate me around here, and I don't know why."

Simon looked surprised. "You don't?" he said. "Well, it's obvious, isn't it? The things you've been saying about people have hurt their feelings."

"What things?" Stevie asked suspiciously.

Simon shrugged. "You know," he said. "All that stuff about her being better than us because she's got a royal title."

Lisa gasped. She and her friends hadn't said a word about Tessa's title to anyone at Pine Hollow. And she was quite sure that Tessa hadn't mentioned it, either.

Simon wasn't finished. "People seem to think she's been making fun of everyone and everything here," he said. He blushed. "For instance, Adam told me that Betsy told him that she heard Theresa thinks I ride like a sack of flour."

"But I would never say something like that!" Tessa protested. "Really, Simon. I'm not that sort of person!"

He shrugged uncertainly. "Well, I must admit, Theresa, I thought you were nice. But some of the things I've heard . . ."

"What else?" Carole asked. "What did Tessa supposedly say about other people here?"

"Oh, I don't like to gossip," Simon protested.

Stevie took a step forward. "Tell us," she said ominously, slapping a bridle hook against her palm.

Simon gulped. "Well, if you insist, Stephanie," he said. "Um, I heard she was making jokes about Jessica Adler being a latchkey kid. And about Betsy's new haircut. Oh, yes, and about Britt being so shy."

Lisa couldn't believe even Veronica could be so mean. She had figured out exactly what each person was sensitive about and made people think that Tessa was ridiculing it. "That's horrible!" she blurted before she could stop herself.

Tessa's face was turning red. "You have to tell me more, Simon," she said evenly. "I want to know everything I'm supposed to have said. That's the only way I'll be able to apologize to everyone."

Before Simon could respond, a familiar voice interrupted. "Hello, everyone!" Veronica was standing in the doorway with a self-satisfied smirk on her face.

Tessa rushed over to her before her friends could stop her. "Just the person I was hoping to see!" she cried. "How dare you tell all these lies about me!"

Veronica shrugged lazily. "I'm sure I don't know what you're talking about." She examined her perfectly manicured fingernails. "I have better things to do than talk about you, believe me."

"Oh, really?" Tessa spat out. "Then how does everyone at Pine Hollow know about my title?"

"Hey, don't blame me for your own bragging," Veronica replied with another shrug.

Tessa was fuming. "And why does everyone think I've been making fun of them? It must have taken you hours to come up with all those lies!"

"Well, that just proves it wasn't me," Veronica said smoothly. "I've spent the last two hours with Miles Pennington, helping him take care of his grandmother's Cleveland Bays." She smiled dreamily. "He just *insisted* on my hanging around and keeping him company the whole time he was here." She patted her smooth, dark hair. "I know he's a little older than me, but I think we have a lot in common."

Carole rolled her eyes. The last thing she felt like doing was listening to the details of Veronica's latest crush—especially since Miles Pennington's family wealth and prestige probably had a lot more to do with it than his looks or personality.

"We all know you did this because you don't like me!"

94

Tessa exclaimed. "You made up those rumors, and you told everyone I thought I was better than them because of my family."

"Why would I do that?" Veronica said calmly. "As far as I'm concerned, your royal connections are the only interesting thing about you. Why would I make fun of something like that? It's just not like me." She smiled an infuriating smile. "Ask anyone."

Carole gasped. She knew that Veronica was lying. But her argument also made a frightening sort of sense. Everyone knew that Veronica was impressed by socially important things like royal titles. What if she could convince other people—Max, for instance—that that meant she was innocent?

As much as Carole wanted to throttle Veronica, she knew there was only one thing to do. "Never mind, Tessa," she said wearily. "There's no point in arguing. Just ignore her."

"So did everyone believe her?" Carole asked the next morning.

Stevie nodded. She and Carole were in the student locker room changing into their riding clothes. "I think so," she said, digging around in her messy cubby in search of her left glove. "But it's a good thing Tessa is so naturally charming. I'm not sure anyone else could have pulled it off."

The day before, Tessa had allowed her friends to convince her to forget about getting back at Veronica. But she hadn't been able to forget about what Veronica had done. She had insisted on tracking down and speaking to every person who had heard the rumors. Carole had left Pine Hollow early for a dentist's appointment, and then she and her father had gone to visit some friends of the family, so she hadn't heard until now how it had turned out.

"I hope Tessa is feeling better about it all today," Carole said, grabbing her boot off the bench beside her. "I'd hate it if this ruined her visit."

"Me too," Stevie agreed. She glanced at her watch. "She and Lisa should be here soon. Listen, before they get here, I was thinking about our vow not to tell her about the probation. Do you think—"

"There you two are!" Lisa's anxious voice interrupted. She and Tessa came rushing into the room. "Listen, we have some terrible news. Tessa can't ride in the junior hurdle race!"

Carole and Stevie gasped. "What?" they exclaimed in one voice.

Tessa gulped. "It's not that bad," she protested. "I keep telling you, Lisa, I don't mind. Really."

"What happened?" Stevie demanded.

Lisa sighed. "It's my mother's fault, as usual," she said. "Well, at least partly. She had lunch with Mrs. diAngelo yesterday, and she blabbed about showing Tessa the map."

"Oh no!" Carole cried. The Saddle Club knew Mrs. diAngelo. She was just an older version of Veronica—selfish and shallow.

"That wouldn't even have been so bad," Lisa went on grimly. "Believe it or not, Mrs. diAngelo was willing to let it go. But then Veronica convinced her it would be better for everyone if Tessa was a judge instead of riding in the race." She shrugged. "By the time we heard about it last night after the evening committee meeting, it was all settled."

Carole could hardly believe it. She couldn't even imagine how disappointed she would be in Tessa's place. "I'm so sorry, Tessa," she said. "This is awful."

"Oh, it's not so bad," Tessa replied, obviously trying to sound like her usual chipper self and failing miserably. "Being a judge will be fun, too."

Suddenly Stevie jumped to her feet. "Enough is enough," she snapped. Before the others could stop her, she stormed out of the room.

"Uh-oh," Carole said.

Lisa was already heading after Stevie. "Double uh-oh," she said. "Let's go!"

They caught up to Stevie in the tack room. Veronica was there, too, backed up against a wall beside the sink.

"You can't do this to our friend and get away with it!" Stevie was yelling. She was holding a large bucket full of soapy, dirty water above her head.

"Stevie!" Lisa hissed, glancing anxiously at the door that led from the tack room to Mrs. Reg's office. "No!"

Stevie didn't even bother to look at her friends. "I hope you brought a change of clothes, Veronica," she snapped.

"You wouldn't dare," Veronica replied haughtily, crossing her arms across her chest.

"Oh, wouldn't I?" Stevie lowered the bucket a little and heaved it back, preparing to splatter its contents all over Veronica.

At that very second Max rushed in from the office. "What's all the shouting in here?" he demanded. He quickly took in the scene, including Stevie and the bucket. "Stevie, what are you doing?"

Stevie shifted her aim just in time. The soapy water splashed harmlessly into the sink. "What do you mean, Max?" she asked innocently. "I was just dumping this out so that I could clean the bucket."

Veronica scowled. "Yeah, right," she muttered. She shoved past the other girls and hurried out of the room.

Max looked suspicious. "Well, keep it down," he said grumpily. Then he left, too.

"Whew," Carole said a little shakily, leaning against a nearby trunk. "That was a close one. We're just lucky Veronica didn't stick around and tattle to Max that—" Suddenly she realized what she had just said. "Oops," she added, glancing at Tessa.

Carole looked at Lisa, then at Stevie. "Listen," she began hesitantly. "Um, I know we haven't talked about this, but . . ."

Lisa was already nodding, looking relieved. "But maybe we should tell Tessa the truth," she finished.

"Tell Tessa the truth about what?" Tessa asked.

"Stevie?" Carole said. "What do you think?"

"I think we should have told her days ago," Stevie

admitted with a sigh. She turned to Tessa. "Something happened right before you got here," she began. Then, with some help from Carole and Lisa, she explained everything—the school assembly, the water balloon prank, the incident with the Penningtons, Max's probation, everything.

By the time the whole story was out, Tessa was grinning. "Wow," she said. "That explains a lot."

"We know," Lisa said wryly. "You were probably wondering why we were letting Veronica get away with all that stuff she's been pulling."

"I sure was," Tessa agreed. "I suppose I should have suspected something was up when you kept refusing to play tricks on her or even raise your voices to her. I should've known you couldn't have changed *that* much since you came to England!"

The other girls laughed, relieved that Tessa wasn't angry with them for keeping secrets.

"So what do we do now?" Carole asked, glancing at the empty water bucket, which Stevie was still holding.

Stevie set the bucket down under the sink. "What can we do?" she said. "Veronica has us just where she wants us. She can do anything she wants, and we can't stop her, because if we try anything she'll tell Max."

"Would Max really revoke your riding privileges?" Tessa asked.

Lisa shrugged. She had been wondering the same thing. After all, she and her friends were normally well-behaved and helpful around the stable. They took good care of the horses they rode, and they were always willing to pitch in and help with the stable chores. In fact, Lisa would have been willing to bet that she, Carole, and Stevie were among Max's favorite people.

Still, she knew that Max had gotten genuinely annoyed by some of Stevie's wilder pranks. He might actually decide to put his foot down to teach them a lesson.

"I don't know," Lisa said. "He might not go through with it. Then again, he might."

"And you can't take that chance." Tessa nodded. "I understand."

Stevie sighed and leaned against the edge of the sink. "I just wish Veronica wasn't being so obnoxious to you during your visit," she told Tessa. "That's the hardest thing to put up with!"

"I know," Tessa said sympathetically. "But you can't let her get to you. Don't worry, I can stand up for myself—especially now that I know the score." She smiled and winked conspiratorially.

Carole smiled back at her. "We know you can. I guess that's why it took us so long to tell you the truth. Boy, were we dumb to think we shouldn't tell you."

"It's just too bad Veronica was able to ruin your chances of riding in the point-to-point," Lisa said sadly.

"Isn't there any chance of changing the committee's mind?" Stevie asked.

Lisa and Tessa both shook their heads. "I doubt it," Lisa

said. "Especially since it sounds as if Mrs. diAngelo is all excited about having Tessa as a judge." She rolled her eyes. "Naturally, Veronica filled her in on Tessa's royal connections, too."

Tessa shrugged, looking resigned. "Really, don't fret," she told her friends. "It's a disappointment, but there's nothing to be done. Watching you ride will be fun. And we can cheer on the riders in the adult races together, right? I don't have to judge those."

"Okay," Lisa said. "You're right. Besides, the best revenge of all will be to ignore Veronica and have fun in spite of her."

Stevie looked doubtful about that, but she nodded. "Maybe you can stick a carrot out in front of Danny's nose when he goes over your jump, Tessa," she suggested jokingly. "Then he'll get distracted and Veronica will lose."

They were all still laughing about that when Veronica walked back into the tack room. Miles Pennington was right behind her, looking handsome in a spotless white polo shirt.

Veronica wrinkled her nose in distaste when she saw the other girls. "Oh," she said to Miles. "It's a little crowded in here. Let's come back later." She grabbed his arm and started to pull him away.

But Miles stood his ground. "Hey, aren't you Tessa?" he said. "I heard you're going to be a fence judge at the point-to-point. I'm going to be one, too."

"Brilliant," Tessa responded. She smiled warmly and stepped forward to offer her hand. "I'm sure it will be lots of fun. By the way, I've been wanting to tell you and your grandmother how interesting that talk about carriage driving was. Your team is gorgeous."

"Thanks. I'll be sure to tell Grandmother that you said so." Miles looked pleased.

Veronica definitely did not look pleased. "Come on, Miles," she whined, still tugging on the teenager's arm. "I thought you wanted to take a walk."

"Just a second," Miles said without glancing around.

Stevie hid a smile. Veronica obviously had a huge crush on Miles Pennington. And he was obviously completely oblivious to that fact. Stevie shot a glance at Carole and Lisa, who looked just as amused as she felt.

Miles didn't notice that, either. "I know Grandmother had a great time showing off the Bays at your meeting," he said to all the girls. "She loves to talk about driving. She's just as enthusiastic about it as she ever was about show jumping."

"Oh, that's right," Carole said, suddenly looking interested in something other than Veronica's annoyance. "We heard she used to win a lot of ribbons in the show-jumping ring."

"She did," Miles confirmed. "But when her arthritis got too bad for her to ride comfortably, she decided she'd rather sit behind a horse than not be anywhere near them." He smiled, his voice fond. "Now she has two

103

teams in training, half a dozen vintage carts and buggies, and a mantel full of driving trophies. And the rest is history."

"Oh, she has a second driving team?" Carole asked. "Are they Cleveland Bays, too? Are they going to stay at Pine Hollow?"

"I don't know if they'll come here or not," Miles replied. "They're boarding temporarily at a friend's farm up in Pennsylvania. I guess they'll probably stay there until our barn is finished, unless Grandmother decides she misses them too much. And no, they're not Bays. They're—"

"Miles," Veronica interrupted. She looked truly annoyed. "I thought you wanted to talk to Max about bringing your friends riding this weekend. We really should go find him."

Miles nodded agreeably. "Okay," he told Veronica. But he paused to explain to the other girls. "A bunch of guys are coming down—friends of mine from the stable where I rode back home in Pennsylvania. They're staying for the weekend, and I thought I'd bring them here for a trail ride if it's okay with Max."

"That sounds nice," Lisa said. "I'm sure Max won't mind a bit." She was glad Miles was being so friendly and not just because it was driving Veronica crazy. She hoped it also meant that he and his grandmother really weren't still mad about the water balloon attack.

Tessa nodded. "There's just one problem," she joked

brightly. "Once your friends ride here, they'll probably never want to go home."

"Oh, really?" Veronica said in a nasty tone. "I hope that's not the case with you, Tessa. By the way, your shirt's missing a button." With that, she flounced out of the room.

Tessa glanced down at the front of her shirt. Meanwhile Miles looked a little surprised, but he didn't say anything about Veronica's rude comments. "Well, goodbye, all," he said lamely, backing out of the room. He grinned weakly. "Cheerio, as they say in England."

"Do they really say that in England?" Lisa asked once Miles had disappeared.

Tessa didn't answer. She was fingering the empty buttonhole near the bottom of her shirt and staring into space with narrowed eyes. "That girl really gets my goat," she muttered.

"No kidding," Stevie said wholeheartedly. "It's bad enough when she insults us. How dare she be so obnoxious to you? We've got to put a stop to it."

Just then Max walked past the open doorway. When he noticed The Saddle Club, he paused. "If you girls are bored, there are some stalls that could use a good cleaning," he said warningly. "And the grain has to be mixed for next week, and the pony harness hasn't been oiled in a while . . ."

"Oh, we're not bored, Max," Stevie said. Max hated seeing his riders standing around doing nothing when

105

there was always so much to be done around the stable. If they didn't act fast, he would set them to work on an endless string of stable chores—guest or no guest. She quickly grabbed Belle's bridle off the wall behind her. "We were just on our way out to practice for the point-to-point." *Even though Tessa can't even ride in it now*, she added in her head. She gave Max her most winning smile.

"Well, all right then," Max said, watching as the other girls also began gathering their tack. "As long as you're keeping busy." He continued on his way.

Lisa let out a sigh of relief. "That was close," she said, rubbing a spot of lint off Derby's browband. She glanced at Stevie. "And by the way, in case you've forgotten, *that's* why we can't put a stop to Veronica's reign of terror. If we do anything to get back at her, she'll tattle."

"And then we can all kiss the point-to-point good-bye," Carole added, hoisting Starlight's saddle off its rack.

Stevie sighed. "I guess you're right," she muttered, looking unhappy. "If we get banned, Veronica wins—no matter what we do."

"You know," Tessa said slowly, "if you think about it, you three are the only ones in danger here. I'm not on probation, am I?"

Carole pretended to be insulted. "Hey, what happened to The Saddle Club motto—all for one and one for all?"

"I thought that was the motto of the Three Muske-teers," Lisa put in.

Tessa grinned. "Don't worry, I'm not abandoning you,"

she said. "Quite the contrary. It just occurred to me—there's nothing to say that I couldn't do something myself to get back at Veronica. It just can't be anything that could be blamed on the three of you. Right?"

"Right," Stevie said, looking intrigued. "What do you have in mind?"

"I don't know yet," Tessa admitted. She grinned and tapped her forehead with one finger. "But from this moment on, the British branch of The Saddle Club is on the case."

THE NEXT MORNING Stevie looked up from Belle's water bucket, listening to footsteps coming down the aisle. A moment later Lisa and Tessa poked their heads into the stall.

"Did you think of anything?" Stevie demanded eagerly.

Tessa laughed. "Is that how you greet all your friends?" she asked.

Stevie grinned. "Nope," she replied, hanging the bucket carefully in its spot on the side wall of Belle's stall. "Just the ones who are going to save us from you-know-who." She winked and lowered her voice to a whisper. "Veronica's in Danny's stall."

Lisa glanced down the aisle and rolled her eyes. "Ugh. You mean we might actually run into her?"

"Only if we're unlucky," Stevie said. She returned her voice to its normal level. "So when is your mom expecting us?"

"An hour ago," Lisa replied. "But that's okay. I told her we'd be there as soon as we finished up here." The four girls had agreed to spend the day helping Mrs. Atwood with her plans for the point-to-point. After her error regarding the course map, she was more nervous than ever about her duties—especially the ones that had anything to do with horses.

"Where's Carole?" Tessa asked, glancing into Starlight's stall, which was right next to Belle's. The friendly bay was watching them curiously, munching on a mouthful of fresh hay. There was no sign of his owner.

"Out in the grain shed, I think," Stevie said, letting herself out of the stall. "Belle's all set. I'll go see if Carole's almost ready while you guys check on Prancer and Topside."

"And Derby," Lisa added. She chuckled. "Until after the point-to-point, I'm on double duty."

Stevie nodded and headed down the aisle. After a few steps, she stopped. "Oh, I almost forgot," she called to the others. "I talked to Phil last night. He wants to get together tomorrow. I thought we could all meet at that new pizza place, Papa's, after lessons. What do you think?"

"Sounds good to me," Lisa called back.

Tessa gave a thumbs-up sign. "I can't wait to meet him," she added.

Stevie smiled as she turned to continue on her way. Her gaze fell on Danny's stall. She wasn't sure, but she thought she saw Veronica ducking out of sight behind the stall door.

Stevie rolled her eyes. Whatever Veronica was up to, she couldn't care less. Tessa would deal with her soon enough. Whistling off-key, Stevie went to find Carole.

"WOW," CAROLE SAID several hours later. She leaned back in her seat at the Atwoods' dining room table and wearily pushed her hair out of her eyes. "Who knew being a member of the country club was so much work?"

Stevie looked up from the Parking sign she was lettering. "What do you mean?" she said. "*We're* the ones doing all the work here. And none of us are members."

Tessa laughed. "Come now, Stevie," she chided. "You know very well that Mrs. Atwood has been working like a demon. At least she has since I've been here. I've barely seen her."

Lisa nodded. Tessa was right. Now that she thought about it, it was probably lucky for The Saddle Club that the point-to-point fell at the end of Tessa's visit. Otherwise they probably would have had to endure a lot more tea parties with her mother.

She pushed her chair back. She had rolled the desk with the family's computer on it into the dining room to be able to work with her friends. Her mother had asked her to update and alphabetize some of the lists and charts

110

for the point-to-point. There were the entrants, the prize sponsors, the presenters, the fence judges . . . Lisa couldn't believe how much information went into a seemingly simple day of races.

"It's hard to believe Max plans events at Pine Hollow all the time," she mused, stretching her arms above her head to rest her back. "Gymkhanas, Pony Club rallies, all those sorts of things."

Carole looked up. "He doesn't do it all alone," she pointed out. "He has lots of help. Mrs. Reg, Red, Deborah . . ." Deborah was Max's wife.

"And us," Stevie added, capping the pen she was using. "We always help him. Just like we're helping your mom now."

At that moment the doorbell rang. "I'd better get that," Lisa said. "I think Mom's on the phone."

She got up and headed for the front door. When she swung it open, she saw a short, stocky man in a dark uniform standing on the front steps. He looked vaguely familiar, but for a moment Lisa couldn't place him. "Can I help you?" she asked politely.

The man gave a little bow. He was holding an ivory-colored envelope in one hand. "Good day, miss," he said in a formal tone. "I have a message for a Miss Theresa from Mrs. diAngelo."

Suddenly Lisa remembered where she had seen the little man before—behind the wheel of the diAngelos' shiny black Mercedes. He was their chauffeur. She glanced out over the front yard and saw the big car parked at the curb. "A message for Tessa?" she repeated. "Okay, thanks. I'll give it to her."

The chauffeur handed the envelope over with a flourish, bowed once more, and turned to go.

As Lisa closed the door behind him, she cast a curious look at the envelope. Tessa's name was written on the front in curly script.

"Who was that, dear?" Mrs. Atwood's voice came from nearby.

Lisa looked up and saw her mother hurrying down the stairs. "The diAngelos' chauffeur just dropped off an envelope for Tessa," she said. "I guess it must be something about her judging or something."

"Oh, my," Mrs. Atwood said. "Well, you'd better give it to her so she can open it right away. It's probably important."

Lisa hurried into the dining room with her mother on her heels. She handed Tessa the envelope, explaining where it had come from.

"Weird," Stevie said. "Are you sure it's from Mrs. diAngelo and not Veronica? Because it might be a letter bomb or something."

Mrs. Atwood shot Stevie a disapproving glance, then smiled at Tessa. "Open it, dear," she urged.

Tessa slit the envelope open with the pencil she had been using. She pulled out a piece of thick paper the same color as the envelope and scanned it. "Oh," she said flatly. "There's a meeting of all the judges at the di-Angelos' house. Tomorrow afternoon."

Stevie glanced over her shoulder and gasped. "But it starts at almost the exact same time we're supposed to meet Phil!" she protested.

Tessa nodded. "I'll have to call Mrs. diAngelo and tell her I can't make it."

Mrs. Atwood looked shocked. "Oh, you mustn't do that!" she exclaimed. "I'm sure the meeting won't take long. And your friends will understand if you're a little late for your pizza party." She frowned slightly. "I don't remember hearing about a judges' meeting," she muttered. "I must have forgotten to put it on my schedule."

Tessa was looking at the note again. "There's a dress code," she said. "There's a line at the end saying I should wear whatever I'm planning to wear to the judges' reception afterward, so they can make sure it's appropriate for this sort of social event." She grimaced. "Whatever that means."

"Oh dear," Mrs. Atwood said, her hands fluttering worriedly. "I do hope you've brought something that will do, Tessa. If not, I'm sure we could squeeze in a quick trip to the mall, and—"

"No, no," Tessa broke in hurriedly. "Mum packed my suitcase, and she always throws in everything but the kitchen sink. I'm sure there's a nice dress or two in there."

"Does that mean you're going?" Stevie was dismayed. "But Phil—"

"Of course she's going," Mrs. Atwood said firmly. "I'm sure she'll be finished in plenty of time for pizza. I'll pick her up and drive her there myself if you like."

"It's all right, Stevie," Tessa said. "Phil won't mind if I'm a bit late, will he?"

"I guess not," Stevie said. But she didn't sound very happy about it.

"Good." Mrs. Atwood seemed relieved. "Would you like me to call Mrs. diAngelo for you and confirm?"

"That's all right," Tessa said politely. "I can do it. The number's right here on the note." She headed for the kitchen.

Lisa followed her. "What a bummer," she said as Tessa picked up the receiver. "Leave it to a diAngelo to mess up our plans."

"At least the meeting's not on Friday. That would mess things up even more," Tessa said. The Saddle Club had been planning all week to take Tessa into nearby Washington, D. C., on Friday to show her the sights. "Stay here while I call," she added. "If Mrs. diAngelo's anything like her daughter, I may need moral support."

Lisa grinned and leaned on the counter beside Tessa. She was close enough to hear when Veronica answered on the other end of the line. "Yes?"

Tessa cleared her throat. "Er, Veronica?" she said in her

most polite voice. "This is Tessa. I was wondering—is your mum in?"

Lisa leaned closer so that she wouldn't miss anything.

"My what?" Veronica replied. "Oh. You must mean my *mom*." She stressed the vowel. "What do you want to talk to her for?" She switched to an exaggerated baby voice. "Are you going to tell her I was mean to you?"

Lisa gritted her teeth. Somehow Tessa maintained her polite, cheerful tone. "Actually, she asked me to come to a meeting of the judges for the point-to-point," she explained. "I was just calling to confirm."

"Oh." That seemed to shut Veronica up for a second. "Hold on. I'll see if she's here."

Tessa put one hand over the receiver as there was a loud clatter of the phone being dropped on the other end. "What a charming girl," she muttered sarcastically, crossing her eyes and sticking out her tongue.

Lisa giggled. That was one of the things she loved about Tessa—she could act like a perfect young lady one second and a total goof the next.

After a couple of minutes Veronica returned to the phone. "Are you still there?" she demanded sullenly.

"I'm here," Tessa replied.

"Mom's in a bubble bath," Veronica said. "She can't come to the phone. But she said you can consider yourself confirmed."

"All right, thanks," Tessa said. "Um, did she happen to

115

mention how long the meeting will take? I'm supposed to be somewhere afterward."

Veronica sighed noisily. "I suppose you want me to go find out," she snapped. "I'm not your servant." Before Tessa could respond, there was another clatter as Veronica dropped the phone.

Carole stuck her head into the kitchen. "What's going on?" she asked. "You left me alone in there with Stevie, and she's muttering all sorts of things about how sorry Veronica is going to be as soon as our probation is over. It's making me kind of nervous."

Lisa giggled. "Well, speaking of Veronica—"

"Hush," Tessa hissed. "I hear footsteps returning."

This time Lisa and Carole both huddled around the phone.

"She said it won't take long," Veronica said abruptly at her end. "Probably about half an hour." She paused, then snorted. "She even said our chauffeur can drive you wherever you need to go afterward. In fact, she suggested you ride home with me from Pine Hollow after lessons." She spoke slowly on this last part, as if the very words pained her. Carole had to clap one hand over her mouth to stifle a giggle.

"Brilliant!" Tessa exclaimed. "That's so nice of her."

"Yeah," Veronica snapped back. She let out a short laugh. "I, for one, can't wait to see what kind of outfit you're planning to wear to this thing. I just hope you haven't been taking wardrobe tips from your Slobbo Club friends. Or with my luck, Mom will make me lend you some clothes." There was a sudden click and then a dial tone.

"Wow." Carole laughed. "It sounds like somebody's not very happy that you're coming to visit."

Tessa rolled her eyes. "The only one less happy about it is me." She frowned. "And how dare she make fun of my wardrobe? Wearing expensive clothing doesn't make one stylish, you know." Her eyes flashed angrily. "I have half a mind to go all posh and make her eat her words."

Her friends smiled sympathetically and headed back into the dining room.

Stevie looked up. "Oh," she said blankly. "Where did you all go?"

Tessa quickly filled her in, doing a pretty good imitation of Veronica's snotty responses. "So it's all set," she finished. "Their driver will even drop me at the pizza place, so I won't miss much." She smiled wryly. "Now all I have to do is pick out which cutoff jeans and tank top I'm going to wear."

Lisa laughed. "What happened to putting her in her place by showing her how a real English lady dresses?" she teased.

Stevie sat bolt upright. "That's a great idea!" she exclaimed. "Make her eat her obnoxious words for once. It would totally kill her if you went to her house dressed better than she was."

"Hmmm," Tessa said, looking thoughtful. A mischievous smile started to play around the corners of her mouth. "Now that you mention it, I suppose that *could* be fun . . ."

"DON'T WRINKLE IT," Lisa warned, reaching out to help Tessa hang an overstuffed garment bag from a hook in the student locker room.

"Don't worry," Stevie put in with a grin. "A few wrinkles aren't going to make any difference. In that outfit, Tessa is going to look so fantastic for that stupid meeting that the diAngelos will be blinded by her!"

"Are you sure we didn't go a bit too far?" Tessa asked worriedly, glancing at the bag. "It's a bit dressy."

Stevie waved one hand airily. "It's perfect," she insisted. "Veronica and her mother don't know the meaning of the word *overdressed*. They'll think it's a compliment."

Carole smiled reassuringly at Tessa. "Don't worry," she said. "The only people who will see you in it are Veronica and a few of her fellow snobs." She held up the department store shopping bag she was carrying. "You can change back into your normal clothes before you come to meet us for pizza."

Other students started to trickle in to get ready for the lesson, so the girls changed the subject. Most of the other students at Pine Hollow seemed to have forgotten all about Veronica's rumors, but a few still gave Tessa odd looks once in a while. The girls didn't want to give anyone any further cause for suspicion. They chatted about the point-to-point and other things as they pulled on their riding boots. Then they headed for the tack room.

Mr. French, the rider who worked for the State Department, was standing in the hallway. "Oh, hello," he said cheerfully when he saw them. "Is this your British friend I've been hearing so much about?"

"Hi, Mr. French," Lisa said. "Yes, this is Tessa." She quickly made the appropriate introductions.

Mr. French shook Tessa's hand. "Well, you don't look like a spy, young lady."

"I beg your pardon?" Tessa said with a smile.

Mr. French chuckled. "I must admit, I don't quite get the joke myself," he said jovially. "But someone's been leaving little notes in my horse's stall warning me that you're a British spy trying to find out American military secrets." He chuckled again and shook his head. "You kids are always joking around. It certainly keeps things lively around here."

Stevie managed to wait until Mr. French had bid them good-bye and wandered off before she exploded. "She's at it again!" she cried. "Doesn't she ever give up?"

"Why should she?" Lisa answered grimly. "She knows we can't stop her."

"Forget it, Stevie," Tessa said. "If that ridiculous spy story is the best she can do, I think I'm safe. Anyway, we've got a plan now, remember?"

Stevie nodded. "Right," she said, clenching her fists.

119

"And now I really can't wait to see Veronica's face when you get into her car looking like a million bucks."

Tessa grinned. "Make that a million pounds," she corrected in an exaggerated upper-crust accent.

AFTER THEIR LESSON was over and their horses were put away, the girls hustled Tessa into the bathroom for her makeover. Carole even remembered to bring a large, clean horse sheet to put over Tessa's outfit when she was ready.

"We can smuggle you out so nobody sees you," she explained.

Tessa nodded. "Good," she said. "The last thing I need is for everyone here to see me looking like some kind of posh society princess. Then they'll really hate me."

"No one hates you," Lisa assured her as she pulled a comb out of the bag. "Well, no one except Veronica. And that's practically a compliment, if you think about it."

It didn't take long for Tessa to get dressed and fix her hair. Soon she stepped back and twirled around in front of the bathroom mirror, looking satisfied. "Well?" she asked. "What do you think?"

Stevie did her best wolf whistle. "Awesome," she said happily. "You'll knock Veronica's one-hundred-percent cashmere socks off."

Tessa did look wonderful. She was dressed in a shimmering silk dress and tastefully sparkling jewelry. Her hair was swept up on top of her head and fastened with a fancy

120

comb. Her patent leather high-heeled shoes were polished and spotless. Overall, she was the very picture of a proper, wealthy young lady dressed to impress.

"Wonderful," Carole said. "You look totally snooty."

Tessa stuck out her tongue. It only ruined the effect a little bit. "Thanks a lot," she said. "Come on, I'd better hurry. I don't want the limo to leave without me!"

Lisa helped Tessa wrap herself in the sheet. Stevie and Carole went out first to make sure the coast was clear. Before long all four girls were outside checking for the diAngelos' car.

"There it is," Lisa said, spotting the Mercedes and chauffeur pulling up. She pulled the sheet back and winked at Tessa. "Have fun."

Tessa gave a rather unladylike snort. "Right," she said sarcastically. She took a deep breath. "Oh, well, stiff upper lip and all that British sort of rot. I'll see you at the pizza place as soon as I can."

Stevie shoved the bag containing Tessa's normal clothes into her hand. "Don't forget this," she said. "We'll try to keep Phil from eating all the pizza before you get there."

Tessa took the bag and tossed her friends a mock salute. The others stood and watched as she headed toward the Mercedes at a stately walk befitting her appearance. She was almost there when Veronica emerged from the stable and spotted her.

"Here we go," Stevie breathed eagerly.

Veronica stared at Tessa for a moment with a surprised look on her face. Then she glanced down at her own expensive but plain black breeches and white shirt. She scowled and hurried toward the car. Tessa smiled at her, but Veronica didn't even meet her glance. She just climbed into the backseat and slammed the door.

"That was sweet," Stevie said with satisfaction as the car pulled away a moment later.

"Sweet enough to make up for cleaning Tessa's tack?" Carole teased. The three friends had offered to finish Tessa's stable chores. They had plenty of time before they had to leave to meet Phil.

They headed to the tack room and got to work. After a few minutes, someone wandered in and greeted them politely.

It was Miles Pennington. "Oh, hello," Lisa said, surprised. "What are you doing here? Shouldn't you be at the diAngelos'?"

The older boy looked confused. "What do you mean?"

"There's a judges' meeting for the point-to-point today," Carole explained. "Tessa just left."

Miles shrugged. "I didn't hear anything about a meeting," he said. "Maybe Mrs. diAngelo forgot to call me."

"She didn't call Tessa," Stevie said. "She sent her a written invitation." She frowned. "Hey, now that I think about it, that's a little weird, even for Mrs. diAngelo."

"Maybe she did it because of Tessa's title," Carole

guessed. "That makes people like her go a little crazy sometimes. Just look at Veronica."

"Maybe," Stevie said. She was starting to get a nervous feeling in the pit of her stomach, though she wasn't quite sure why. "Or maybe something even stranger is going on here."

"Come on, Stevie," Lisa protested a little while later as the three girls hopped off the bus in front of Papa's Pizza Palace. "Mrs. diAngelo may be strange, but she'd never agree to help Veronica kidnap Tessa. That's a ridiculous theory even for you."

Stevie didn't answer. "I hope Phil and A.J. are here," she said instead, hurrying up the walk to the front door of the pizza place. "They have pretty devious minds. Maybe they can help us figure out what Veronica is up to."

Once they got inside, the girls spotted Phil and his best friend, A.J., right away. They were saving a large table in the center of the room.

"Hi, A.J." Carole sat down across from the two boys. "Hi, Phil. How was your vacation?"

"Never mind that," Stevie snapped. "Listen, guys. We've got a problem."

"I missed you too, Stevie," Phil joked. "Hey, where's your friend Tessa? I thought that was the main reason we were all getting together."

Lisa was scoping out the restaurant. Papa's had opened just a month earlier, and she had never been there before. The large, cheerful main room was decorated with huge photos of delicious-looking pizza. But that wasn't what Lisa was looking at, even though she was hungry after all the riding she had done that day.

"Hey, check it out," she told her friends, twisting around to look at the tables behind her. "It looks like we weren't the only ones at Pine Hollow who decided to come here today."

Carole turned to look. "You're right," she said in surprise. Betsy Cavanaugh and Meg Durham were crowded into a booth with Adam Levine and Joe Novick, right underneath a huge picture of a pepperoni-and-mushroom pizza. Helen Sanderson was sitting with her brother, Tom, and several friends near the door. Polly, Britt, Anna, and Lorraine were giggling over a large cheese pie. Even some of the younger riders were there—Liam's teenage sister was sitting with Liam and a group of his friends from the beginners' riding class.

"Did Max hand out coupons and we missed it?" Lisa joked.

Stevie looked annoyed. "Who cares about that?" she

125

said. "Aren't you the least bit worried about what Tessa may be going through right now at Veronica's house of horrors?"

"Shhh," Carole warned. "Keep it down. We don't want the whole stable to know what's going on."

Lisa nodded. "Good point," she agreed. "Otherwise it might get back to Max that we're plotting against Veronica, and then . . ." She made a cutting motion across her throat with one finger.

Phil and A.J. were looking from one girl to another, their faces increasingly confused. "What exactly is going on here?" Phil asked plaintively. "Why is Tessa at Veronica's house?"

"Why are you worried that Max will get wind of what you're doing?" A.J. added.

"Why is Stevie drumming her fingers on the table like she does when she's worried about something?" Phil went on.

Carole and Lisa laughed. Stevie just rolled her eyes, but she stopped drumming her fingers and leaned closer to the boys.

"Okay," she said crisply. "Here's the story. Now listen up, and don't interrupt. We may not have much time." She quickly filled them in on everything that had happened in the past week, from their misguided attack against the Penningtons to Tessa's departure for the di-Angelos' house.

"Wow," Phil said when she finished. "What do you think Veronica's—"

At that moment the little bell over the door tinkled as someone came in, and a gasp of surprise went up from the diners facing the door. A second later, everyone was turning and craning their necks to see who had come in.

The Saddle Club turned, too. Lisa gasped. "Tessa!" she exclaimed.

Tessa was standing just inside the door, looking upset as she scanned the familiar faces in the restaurant. She was also looking very posh, as she would have described it. She was still wearing the fancy outfit she had put on to go to the meeting. It was no wonder people were staring— Tessa looked very out of place in the casual atmosphere of the pizza restaurant.

Tessa soon spotted her friends and scurried toward their table, dropping into the empty seat between Carole and Lisa. Her face was red. "You won't believe this one," she muttered, glancing around cautiously.

Lisa looked around, too. She saw that many of the diners had already lost interest and returned to their meals. But not the other Pine Hollow students. Most of them were still shooting curious or disbelieving glances at Tessa and whispering to their friends.

Lisa gulped. This wasn't good. Tessa had almost convinced everyone that she was a nice, normal girl like anyone else. But now here she was, looking just as snooty and regal as could be.

"What happened?" Carole demanded. "Where are your other clothes?"

Before Tessa could answer, the bell over the door tinkled again and Veronica strolled in. She came toward The Saddle Club's table.

"There you are, Tessa," she said casually. "You rushed out of the car so fast I couldn't keep up."

"What do you want, Veronica?" Stevie demanded, glaring at her.

Veronica shrugged. "Oh, I just wanted to apologize to Tessa again," she said smoothly. She turned to Tessa with a fake smile. "I'm so sorry about the little accident with your other clothes. You really shouldn't carry things around in paper bags like that—they're just not waterproof at all." She shrugged. "But I told the servants to fish everything out of the pool and have it dry cleaned. So no harm done, right?" She grinned and left before the others could say anything.

Carole watched with a frown as Veronica sat down with Betsy and her friends. "I think I'm starting to figure out what's going on," she muttered.

"Me too," Stevie said. "And I don't like it." Suddenly remembering the boys, she quickly introduced them to Tessa.

Tessa politely said hello, then sighed. "This is horrible," she said. "Now the entire state of Virginia will think Veronica was right—I'm just a big snob who's looking down her nose at everyone."

"There wasn't any judges' meeting, was there?" Lisa asked.

Tessa shook her head. "Mrs. diAngelo wasn't even home. Veronica set this whole thing up to humiliate me by having me arrive at Papa's dressed like opening night at the opera." She sighed again. "I must admit, she's a better actor than I would have thought. The whole ride over there in the car, I would have sworn she was upset about having me come to her house."

"She's getting sneakier and sneakier," Phil commented. "I bet she made sure all these kids from Pine Hollow would be here, too."

"You can count on that." Stevie looked angry. "She took care of all the details. She even goaded Tessa into dressing up more than she would have normally."

"As soon as my regular clothes 'fell' into the pool—" Tessa began.

"How did Veronica manage that, anyway?" Carole interrupted.

"She insisted on using the phone by the pool to summon the chauffeur for me," Tessa said. "When we were out by the pool, I set the bag down for a second and she 'accidentally' kicked it into the water."

"You should have gone back to Pine Hollow," Stevie

said. "You could have borrowed some of the extra clothes from our cubbies."

"I didn't think of that," Tessa admitted sadly, blinking hard. "Besides, I didn't realize all these people from Pine Hollow would be here. I thought I would just look stupid in front of Phil and A.J. and a bunch of strangers."

Lisa could tell that Tessa was really upset. "It's okay," she said, trying to cheer her up. "Being seen in Stevie's ratty old jeans wouldn't have been any better for your reputation than this, believe me."

Just then a waitress approached their table. "Are you ready to order?" she asked, her pad and pencil at the ready.

Lisa looked over at Tessa. "Do you know what you want?" she asked. "You're the guest of honor, so you can pick the toppings."

Tessa smiled weakly, then rested her head in her hands. "That's okay, you guys go ahead and decide," she said. "I'm not very hungry."

Lisa could tell that even Tessa's natural high spirits were having trouble overcoming this problem. The worst part was, she didn't look angry, as she had after Veronica's other obnoxious pranks and nasty comments. She just looked upset. Lisa could understand that—she was sure that Tessa really hated the thought of everyone thinking she was snobby and full of herself.

But what could they do to cheer her up?

* * *

"STEVIE! PHONE FOR YOU," Stevie's brother Chad shouted later that night. "I think it's Belle. She wants to talk to you about some manure."

"Very funny," Stevie muttered, hurrying into the kitchen and snatching the phone from her brother. "Hello?" she said into the receiver.

"Hi, it's me," Lisa said on the other end of the line. She was talking so quietly that Stevie could hardly hear her.

"Speak up," Stevie said. "How's Tessa?"

"That's why I'm whispering," Lisa replied. "She's in the other room with my mom, and I don't want them to hear me." A noisy sigh came through the phone. "She's still pretty depressed."

Stevie bit her lip and played with the hem of her nightshirt. She had been thinking and thinking about how they could get back at Veronica and cheer up Tessa, but she hadn't come up with a thing.

"I'm really getting kind of worried," Lisa went on. "I'm afraid Tessa might decide to cut her visit short because of this."

Stevie gasped. "Are you serious?" Tessa was supposed to stay through the July Fourth weekend. It would be horrible if Veronica's stupid prank made her go back to England before that.

"Okay, maybe I'm exaggerating," Lisa admitted. "But she sure seems a lot less enthusiastic about riding at Pine

131

Hollow now. She thinks everyone there except us hates her."

"Thanks to you-know-who," Stevie muttered. "We've got to think of a plan!"

"But what can we do?" Lisa asked, sounding hopeless. "If we so much as look cross-eyed at Veronica, she'll go running to Max. And we can kiss our horses good-bye for the rest of Tessa's visit—at least."

Stevie knew she was right, but she didn't like it. "Well, let's keep thinking," she said stubbornly. "Maybe something brilliant will come to us."

"Okay," Lisa said. "By the way, Dad wants to get an early start, so we'll be picking you up around eight-thirty, all right?"

"Oh." Stevie had almost forgotten about the trip to Washington, D.C. For a second she wished they didn't have to go. But once she thought about it, the timing couldn't have been better. Maybe getting away from Willow Creek and Pine Hollow for the day would help Tessa's cheerful personality bounce back. "Okay," she told Lisa. "I'll be ready."

"Great," Lisa said. "I'd better call Carole." She said good-bye and hung up.

Stevie returned the phone to its cradle and wandered out of the kitchen, thinking about their problem. Veronica had succeeded in her goal—she was making Tessa completely miserable. How could the rest of The

Saddle Club stop her before she totally ruined Tessa's trip?

Stevie sighed as she plodded up the stairs. Normally there would be so many things they could do. They could fill Veronica's Pine Hollow cubby with peanut butter. They could sneak into Danny's stall at night and dye him purple or neon pink. They could replace Veronica's expensive riding boots with a pair of flip-flops.

But all of those ideas were impossible now. Lisa was right—it wouldn't take much to make Max carry out his threat to suspend their riding privileges.

Still, Stevie and the others had to do something to help Tessa. They just had to. After all, wasn't that the whole point of The Saddle Club?

Stevie took a deep breath. She had reached a decision. They couldn't just stand by any longer. There was no telling how much worse Veronica's pranks could get. It was time to put a stop to them. And if that meant facing the consequences with Max, then they would just have to live with them.

Stevie felt a little better. She knew she wouldn't be feeling too great when she was banned from riding Belle for weeks and weeks, but she decided to worry about that later. She had some plotting and scheming to do.

She was trying to figure out exactly how much peanut butter it would take to fill an entire cubby when she wandered past the open door to her brother Michael's room.

Loud hoots of laughter coming from inside the room caught her attention.

"What's going on?" she demanded, pausing in the doorway.

Her three brothers looked up at her. Chad and Alex were laughing hysterically. Michael was frowning and looking annoyed.

"Oh, hi, Stevie," Alex choked out. He pointed at Michael and started laughing again. "Remember those?"

Stevie glanced at her younger brother and started to grin as she realized what her other brothers were laughing at. Michael was wearing his weirdest pajamas, which had been a Christmas gift from an eccentric older relative. They were made of bright magenta cotton, which had faded—but not enough!—to a pale pink, and decorated all over with embroidered bunnies and lambs. Stevie knew that Michael had hated the pajamas on sight and had tried to hide or destroy them many times. But their parents had always found them and made him wear them again.

Michael's face was bright red. "Shut up!" he shouted at his laughing siblings. "I had to wear these. All my other pajamas are in the laundry, and Mom made me." He glared at Stevie. "Besides," he added, "that stupid shirt of yours is even worse."

Chad stopped laughing and looked at Stevie's favorite oversized horse T-shirt. "You know, Michael, I think you're right," he said. "Who else but Stevie would keep wearing something until it fell apart into individual molecules just because it happens to have a picture of some stupid horse on it?" Soon all three boys were pointing and laughing at Stevie.

Stevie just rolled her eyes and continued down the hall. She knew her nightshirt had seen better days, but she still liked it. "Boys!" she said in disgust, hurrying into her room. She slammed the door as she heard the sounds of laughter moving out into the hall behind her. With a snort, she thought back to all the times her brothers had crashed Saddle Club sleepovers to make fun of what she and her friends wore to bed. "What's so funny about pajamas, anyway?" she muttered.

Suddenly her eyes widened. She started to grin, ignoring the sounds of her brothers pounding on her door and her father shouting for quiet.

She hurried toward the phone beside her bed. She had to call Carole and Lisa right away. She had just come up with the perfect plan! She didn't have all the details worked out yet, but her mind was clicking along in high gear.

Stevie grinned as she dialed Lisa's number. This would really put Veronica in her place.

But that wasn't even the best part. If everything worked out as Stevie thought it could, Max need never be the wiser!

* * *

"I LOVED THE Smithsonian!" Tessa declared on Saturday morning as The Saddle Club walked into the stable for their Horse Wise meeting. "I'm still thinking about everything we saw yesterday. Where else could you see dinosaur bones, famous spacecraft, lovely paintings, the Hope Diamond, and live insects all in one place?"

"Does that mean you were more impressed by holding that tarantula at the Insect Zoo than by our tour of the White House?" Carole teased. She was happy that Tessa's mood had improved so much since Thursday night. She was sure that their fun-filled day in Washington had had something to do with that. But she was equally certain that Stevie's new plan had done its part as well. The four girls had spent most of their sleepover the night before making plans.

There was one aspect of the plot that still worried Carole, though. "Do you really think we can convince Max to go along with this?" she asked as she and her friends headed for the locker room. "I mean, we're not exactly on his good side these days."

Tessa tossed her head. "He's not mad at me, is he?" she reminded them.

Soon the girls had saddled their horses and were gathered in the outdoor ring with the rest of the class. Max perched on the fence and addressed the group.

"As you can probably guess," he began, "we'll be spending most of today's meeting practicing for next week's point-to-point at the country club. I know most of you are entered in the junior hurdle race, and I also know that this race is going to be a little different than anything you've attempted before. So I want to make sure you're as ready as possible."

"Did you hear that?" Stevie whispered to Carole excitedly. "He's practically playing right into our hands!"

Carole nodded. She was just as excited about that as Stevie. But she was also excited at the thought of competing in the point-to-point. She gave Starlight a pat and then returned her attention to Max.

"Almost all of you have experience jumping in the show ring," he said. "But a race like this is different. It won't just be you and your horse performing out there all alone. You'll be competing directly against lots of other riders. It's probably a lot closer to the fox hunt we held here a while ago than to anything else we've done in Horse Wise."

Tessa raised her hand. "That's very true, Max," she said. "After all, steeplechasing began as a way for hunters to show off their horses."

"She's buttering him up," Stevie whispered gleefully.

Carole nodded. Max was smiling at Tessa and agreeing with what she had said. Then he went on to give a brief history of the sport of steeplechasing, including a lot of the information Tessa had already shared with her friends.

"Steeplechasing isn't nearly as popular here in the U.S. as it is in Great Britain," Max continued. "But its popularity is growing. Several major racetracks hold occasional steeplechases as part of their schedule. American steeplechases are two to two and a half miles long and usually have eleven or twelve jumps."

"Wow," Carole whispered to her friends. "Two and a half miles? That's a lot longer than a regular horse race."

Max went on. "But steeplechases held at racetracks are only one kind of jumping race," he said. "There are a couple of other types. Can anyone guess what one of those is?"

"Point-to-point!" called out several students at once.

Normally Max didn't like his students yelling out answers without raising their hands, but this time he smiled. "Right," he said. "A point-to-point takes place cross-country over natural obstacles. In an old-fashioned style point-to-point, competitors choose their own path from start to finish—point to point—jumping whatever's in their way."

Tessa raised her hand. "That sounds just like that very first race between those two hunters back in Ireland," she said.

"Right," Max agreed. "In fact, even today a point-to-point is thought of as a race for hunters, especially in England. But these days it's more usual for a course to be laid out beforehand with special fences set up. That's what the country club has planned for next Saturday." He smiled. "Although technically, I suppose their program could also come under the third category of jump racing—a hunt race meeting. That's an informal day of half a dozen races or so. It might include flat races as well as jumping ones, over timber or brush obstacles. And sometimes these meetings include restricted races, such as those for young riders only." He smiled. "For example, the junior hurdle race that most of you will be riding in next weekend. The Maryland Hunt Cup is probably the most famous example of a hunt meeting in America."

Tessa raised her hand again. Carole noticed several other members of Horse Wise giving the British girl disgruntled looks. She guessed that Tessa had Veronica to thank for that. Still, she was pretty sure she knew what Tessa was going to say next—and that the other students were going to like it.

"Yes, Tessa?" Max nodded for her to speak.

"I just have one tidbit to add to your history of steeplechasing, if you don't mind," she said. When Max nodded again, she went on. "I told some people about it last week. It was a notorious race known as the Midnight Steeplechase."

Several students nodded as they remembered what Tessa had told them the previous Saturday afternoon. One or two also giggled as they recalled that the racers on that long-ago evening had worn nightshirts over their normal clothing.

But Tessa didn't mention that aspect of the event.

"The race took place among British cavalry officers stationed at Ipswich," she explained instead. "It was held cross-country after dinner one evening."

"That sounds like it was fun," Max said with a smile. "All right, then—"

Stevie couldn't hold back any longer. She had to jump in to make sure their plan worked. "Hey, Max!" she called, leaning forward in her saddle and waving her hand in the air.

Max frowned slightly. "Yes, Stevie?" he said.

"Wouldn't it be fun to have something like that here?" she said brightly. "Maybe we could do it tonight!"

Max laughed. "Sure, Stevie," he replied sarcastically. "Now, as I was saying—"

"Oh, but Max!" Tessa interrupted. "I think it's a marvelous idea to hold our own midnight steeplechase. And it would be terrific practice for next week!"

Max looked surprised. "Well, yes," he said. "I suppose it would be. But I just don't have time to pull something like that together today. I'm sorry."

"We could all help," Carole spoke up. "You wouldn't have to do a thing."

"Definitely!" called out Adam Levine. "It sounds like a blast! I'll help!"

Stevie grinned. All around her, people were chattering excitedly about the idea. Even the horses were shifting their feet as they picked up on the humans' excitement.

Max frowned and scanned his students. Stevie crossed her fingers. He had to say yes. He had to!

Suddenly a new voice rang out. "I think it's a stupid idea," Veronica said loudly. She gave Tessa and the rest of The Saddle Club a dismissive glance. "Who cares what some dumb British soldiers did a million years ago? Riding around the countryside at night isn't my idea of a good time." She shrugged. "Besides, it sounds dangerous." She turned and smiled sweetly at Max. "Aren't you always telling us not to ride fast after dark?"

Lisa jumped in before Max could answer. "It wouldn't actually take place at midnight," she pointed out sensibly. "We're talking about right after dinner. And it doesn't get dark this time of year until late."

"That's true," put in Polly Giacomin, patting her horse. "And Romeo and I could really use some practice. I didn't own him when we held that fox hunt." She glanced at her friend Britt, who was beside her. "And Britt wasn't even riding at Pine Hollow then."

"Neither was I," called out Andrea Barry. "I think a midnight steeplechase could be fun."

"Well," Max said at last, sounding a little grumpy. "It sounds like you've all made up your minds. What else can I do but go along?" He waited a moment for the cheers to die down. "But you're going to have to do all the work," he warned. "It won't be easy to pull this together in one day. Maybe we should hold it next week."

"No, we can do it!" Stevie called out. "I personally volunteer to check with all the property owners around Pine Hollow to get permission to ride over their land tonight. I'll also—um—take care of gathering the—uh—stuff we'll need for the ride."

Max looked confused. But Carole didn't give him a chance to ask any questions. "I'll organize a group to come up with a course," she offered. "Lisa can print out maps on her family's computer."

Several other students quickly volunteered for other tasks. Max shrugged. "Okay, okay," he said, throwing up his hands with a wry smile. "Tonight it is, then. You can get started on your planning right after Horse Wise. Now let's get this meeting started before it's time to end it!"

"HI, TESSA," ANNA McWhirter said, coming over to The Saddle Club as they cleaned their tack after the meeting. "I just wanted to say, that was a great idea you had about the midnight steeplechase. I think it will be fun."

"Thanks," Tessa said, returning the other girl's smile.

As Anna wandered off to hang up her horse's bridle, Lisa leaned over to Tessa. "I guess at least one person decided you weren't too snooty after all," she whispered. She didn't want the other students in the tack room to overhear. There were at least half a dozen riders there busily taking care of their tack. So far several of them had smiled tentatively at Tessa and one or two had actually said hello. Luckily, Veronica's prank seemed to be wearing off.

Tessa beamed. "I know," she whispered back. "I hope it's catching!"

Stevie hadn't heard them. She was thinking about something else. "I told Max after class about the costume part of the story," she said. She shook her head. "I can't believe I almost blurted it out in front of—"

"Shhh!" Carole hissed, gesturing toward the door with her head.

The girls all turned to look. Veronica had just come in, carrying Danny's sweaty saddle and bridle. She dropped the tack on a nearby rack, then surveyed the room with her hands on her hips.

"I can't believe you were all so excited about that silly dinnertime steeplechase idea," she said loudly. She let out a derisive snort. "Let me tell you, I for one have better things to do on a Saturday night."

Stevie frowned. She hadn't anticipated this. Their midnight steeplechase wouldn't exactly be an official Horse Wise function, so they couldn't count on Max making participation mandatory. What if Veronica just refused to ride?

"What's the matter, Veronica?" she said quickly. "Are you scared of losing?"

Veronica rolled her eyes. "Oh, please. I'm in no hurry to beat you, Stevie." She smiled coolly. "I can wait until the point-to-point for that. It will be more fun to do it

143

with half the town watching." She smirked and stared at Tessa. "It's just too bad I won't have the chance to beat your little friend, too, since she's stuck being a judge. Really too bad."

"Oh, really?" Tessa said calmly, standing up. "Well, here's your chance, Veronica. If you ride tonight, we can see who's the better rider once and for all—you or me."

By then, all other conversation in the tack room had ceased. Every student in the place was watching Veronica and Tessa.

Veronica laughed. "I don't need to ride tonight to know that," she replied haughtily.

Tessa glanced at her friends. Then she turned back to face Veronica. "All right, then why don't we make things a bit more interesting . . . with a friendly wager?" she suggested.

Veronica looked around and realized for the first time that she had a sizable audience. "What do you have in mind?" She sounded cautious.

"Well, let's see." Tessa paused to think. "If you finish ahead of me, I'll, um . . ." She turned desperately to her friends for help.

Stevie jumped right in. "If you beat Tessa"—she pointed to Veronica—"Tessa will dress up as a rodeo clown and perform in the Willow Creek Fourth of July parade next Sunday afternoon." She smiled. "And if Tessa beats you, you have to do the same thing."

Veronica hesitated. Carole could almost see her turning

144

the challenge over in her mind, wavering between her malicious desire to make Tessa look like a fool and her equal desire not to take any chances on looking like a fool herself.

"Come on, Veronica," Joe Novick spoke up suddenly, breaking the silence. "What are you, chicken?"

"Chicken!" Adam Levine sang out. He tucked his hands under his armpits and flapped his elbows up and down. *"Buck, buck! Chicken!"* Joe joined in, and soon both boys were dancing around the tack room acting like poultry.

Veronica shot them a look of pure hatred. "Shut up," she snapped. "I'm no chicken." She walked over to Tessa and put out her hand. "It's a bet!"

"Is EVERYTHING READY to go?" Carole asked Stevie that evening.

"Everything except the most important thing," Stevie replied grimly. "Veronica hasn't shown up yet."

Carole finished tightening Starlight's girth. "Uh-oh." She glanced at her watch. "Do you think she decided not to come after all?"

"I sure hope not." Stevie shook her head in dismay. "Everything else is just perfect. Lisa has the special map all ready. And of course, the pajamas I collected are fantastic." She grinned. "Even if Veronica got first pick, she'd still be totally humiliated. There's not a designer original in the box."

Carole laughed. "Well, let's just keep our fingers crossed and hope she turns up," she said. "Did you make that call?"

"It's all taken care of," Stevie assured her.

"Good." Carole led Starlight out of his stall. "I'll see you out there."

Stevie nodded and hurried into Belle's stall next door. The lively mare was already saddled and ready. Stevie had left her tied in the stall for a few minutes while she had gone to see whether Veronica had arrived.

"Are you ready for this, girl?" Stevie asked her horse.

Belle snorted in reply. Stevie took that as a yes.

Stevie led Belle outside. The sun was still up, but a cool breeze was snaking its way through the crowd already gathered in front of the stable building. Most of Horse Wise was there with their horses. Max was standing by to supervise. A large cardboard box was right next to him, filled to the brim with nightclothes. Stevie had been in charge of gathering them, which meant that there wasn't an ordinary set of flannel pajamas in sight.

Betsy Cavanaugh leaned over the box and squealed as she pulled a silky polka-dotted nightgown out of the box. "Do we actually have to wear this stuff?" she cried with a giggle.

"That's how this works," Max replied, looking amused. "Or so they tell me." He winked at Tessa, who was standing nearby at Topside's head. Then he went over to help

Simon Atherton, who had just emerged with Patch in tow. Patch's girth was far too loose, and his saddle was already slipping to the side.

Stevie left Belle tied near the door. Tessa did the same with Topside. Both girls headed for the box. Stevie grinned as more and more riders joined them there, arguing over the best costumes. A few of the riders who hadn't known that the costumes were part of the midnight ride were a little confused at first. But those who had been present when Tessa first told the story soon filled them in. Before long everyone was busy pulling on wacky nightclothes over their jeans and T-shirts. Joe Novick paraded around in a pink-and-green flowered housecoat. Polly and Britt found matching striped nightcaps and a couple of pea green gowns. Betsy pulled on the polka-dotted nightie.

Stevie grabbed a pig-print nightshirt for herself. "Rats," she commented to Tessa, who was digging through the costumes. "I can't believe Joe picked that hideous housecoat. I was hoping Veronica would have to wear that."

"Don't worry." Tessa stretched to reach the bottom of the box. "There are plenty of disgusting options left in here." She pulled out a gauzy purple gown with green lace trim and grinned. "But Veronica can't have this. This is mine!"

Lisa and Carole joined their friends at the box. "Where's Veronica?" Lisa asked worriedly, scrabbling through the costumes for something to wear.

148

"That's exactly what I was wondering," Stevie said.

Tessa looked up from tying a pale orange bed jacket over her purple gown, obviously surprised at Stevie's comment. "Oh, I thought she was here already," she said. "I haven't seen her myself, but when I walked past Danny's stall ten minutes ago, he was all tacked up already."

Stevie, Carole, and Lisa stared at each other. "Red!" they exclaimed in one voice. Then they quickly explained to Tessa what they meant. Veronica nearly always made Red tack up Danny for her. She had even been known to call ahead so that her horse would be ready and waiting when she strolled in. That seemed to be the case today.

"At least that means she's planning to come," Carole said hopefully. She grabbed a bright yellow baby-doll gown with frog-shaped buttons and yanked it over her head.

Stevie nodded. "Actually, it's perfect," she declared. "The less time she has before we start, the less time she has to complain about—"

"What's going on here?" Veronica's shriek cut her off.

The Saddle Club turned to see Veronica striding up the driveway. Her parents' car was just pulling away. Veronica was staring in disbelief at the strangely dressed people around her.

Lisa straightened the frilly white nightcap she'd just jammed onto her own head. "What do you mean, Veronica?" she asked innocently.

Veronica glared. Then she flounced over to Max. "I didn't know this was some kind of pathetic costume parade," she announced. "So I'm afraid I left my hideous outfit at home."

"Don't worry, Veronica," Max replied. He gestured at the box. "We have enough costumes for everyone. You'd better hurry, though—everyone's picked theirs out already. You may be left with the dregs."

"What's the difference?" Veronica stared as Joe danced past her pretending to be a ballerina while Betsy and Meg giggled wildly. "Anyway, you've got to be kidding. There's no way I'm wearing a costume."

Max shrugged and crossed his arms over his chest. "That's your choice," he told her. "But rules are rules. If you don't dress up, you don't ride." He turned away to help one of the younger riders.

Veronica stormed over to The Saddle Club. "You people must think you're awfully funny, don't you?" she snapped. "Well, how's this for a joke? I'm leaving."

"But, Veronica!" Tessa spoke up quickly. "If you don't ride, you forfeit. And you know what that means." She swung an imaginary lasso above her head. *"Yeee-ha!"*

Veronica rolled her eyes. "Yeah, right," she muttered. "I'm out of here."

Stevie gulped. She hadn't considered this possibility. When The Saddle Club had talked it over a couple of hours earlier, they had thought the plan was practically foolproof from then on. Veronica couldn't back out when

150

she found out about the costumes or she would lose the bet. But they had failed to take Veronica's treacherous personality into account. Now it was obvious what would happen—Veronica would just refuse to make good on her end of the deal.

"Uh-oh," she muttered.

"Wait," Lisa whispered. "Tessa predicted this might happen. We came up with a plan on our way over here after dinner. Just play along."

Meanwhile, Veronica had turned to go. But Tessa grabbed her shoulder before she could take a step. "Wait," she ordered.

Veronica shook off her hand and turned back, looking annoyed. "Let go of me," she snapped.

"I think you'll want to hear what I have to say," Tessa said, pushing up the sleeves of her purple gown. "What do you say we up the odds on our little wager?"

Veronica shrugged, not looking very interested. "I doubt you can come up with anything that will make this"—she gestured at the pajama-clad crowd around her—"worth my while."

"How about this?" Tessa said belligerently. She put her hands on her hips. "If I beat you, your punishment stands. But if you somehow manage to beat me, I'll dress up in whatever costume you want and perform in the town parade—*and* at the fireworks afterward." She jerked a thumb at the rest of The Saddle Club. "And so will my friends."

Carole let out a loud gasp. "Are you crazy?" she hissed at Tessa in a stage whisper.

Lisa was backing away. "I don't know about that . . ."

Stevie felt like grinning. Tessa was brilliant! "Hold on a second, Tessa," she said seriously, playing along. "Maybe we should talk about this first."

Veronica couldn't resist. "It's a deal!" she said quickly. She gave a wicked smile. "Wearing a silly nightgown will all be worth it—when I see the four of you making total fools of yourselves in front of the entire town!" She hurried over to the almost empty box. "Okay, what do we have here?"

She bent over and pulled something out. Stevie would have laughed out loud when she saw it if she hadn't still been pretending to be upset with Tessa. Veronica was holding the top half of Michael's fuzzy pink pajamas!

Veronica held the bunny-print nightshirt gingerly between her thumb and forefinger and wrinkled her nose in distaste. "You've got to be kidding," she muttered. She reached into the box again, but all she came up with was a nightcap shaped like a big, fuzzy sheep, complete with aqua blue googly eyes and a protruding pink felt tongue.

"Almost ready, Veronica?" Max asked briskly, hurrying over.

"Not quite," Veronica said. "I can't wear this stuff. If you give me fifteen minutes, I'll call the maid and have her send over one of my decent nightgowns—"

"Forget it," Max cut her off. "We're running late already, and we want to be finished before dark. Put that stuff on and go get Danny. Now!"

For a second Veronica seemed ready to argue. But when Max glared at her, she gave in. "Oh, all right," she muttered, shrugging the too-small faded pink nightshirt on over her short-sleeved red blouse.

"Hold on to that cap," Max insisted as Veronica started to toss the sheep-shaped nightcap back into the box. "I'm sure it will fit over your riding hard hat. And everyone has to wear at least two items. Rules."

Veronica shot him a look of pure disbelief. But Max's expression was serious. Even Veronica knew better than to argue with him when he looked like that. She glanced around again at her fellow riders and finally seemed convinced that everyone else's outfits were just as ridiculous as hers, even taking the sheep hat into consideration. "Fine," she said in exasperation, tucking the woolly cap under her arm.

She headed toward the stable door. On her way, she paused beside The Saddle Club. "Don't worry," she whispered to them. "I may look ridiculous now. But not half as ridiculous as you're all going to look next weekend at that parade!"

"EVERYBODY READY?" Max called.

The riders in the midnight steeplechase were forming a

jagged line on the far side of the outdoor ring, facing the broad, open fields behind Pine Hollow.

Veronica had just mounted. "Hold it," she complained. "Nobody even told me where we're supposed to end up."

Lisa rode over to her and held out a folded piece of paper. "Here's a copy of the map," she said brightly. "We're doing this as an old-fashioned point-to-point, so you have to choose your own route. The first one who gets to the spot marked on the map with an X is the winner."

Max glanced at his watch. "Veronica, you have exactly thirty seconds to look over the map," he announced. "Then we're starting this race. Meanwhile, I just want to remind everyone of a few ground rules. You all know which property owners allow us on their land and which don't. And by the way, I should add that Mrs. Pennington has graciously agreed that we can ride on her property whenever we like, as long as we follow the usual courtesies about leaving gates the way we found them and so forth." He took a breath. "Also, please remember—even though this is a race, that's no excuse for risky riding. Don't go faster than you and your horse are comfortable with. If you don't think you can handle an obstacle, stop and go around it. And don't crowd your fellow riders." He glanced at his watch again. "Got it? Okay, with that said—have fun! Red is already waiting at the finish line. I'll see you there!"

"Here we go!" Carole said. She was feeling excited, and

not only because of their prank. Somehow, being out in the evening air preparing to ride cross-country was even more exciting than she would have thought. The horses seemed to feel it, too. Most of them were tossing their heads or stamping their feet eagerly, despite the fact that it was almost their dinnertime.

"On your marks," Max said, raising one hand above his head. "Get set . . . Go!" His hand fell, and the horses took off.

"There she goes!" Stevie called to her friends as they all lunged forward.

Danny had responded instantly to his rider's command, as usual. That meant that Veronica had a jump on most of the other riders. She immediately aimed him off at a left angle, while the rest of the pack veered to the right.

Stevie was sure that some of the other riders were surprised at Veronica's choice of paths. Come to think of it, if Max was still watching, he was probably surprised, too, since the old stone wall marked with an X on the maps of every other rider was off to the right. She just hoped he put it down to Veronica's poor map skills.

"Come on," Carole shouted, crouching lower over Starlight's back as he broke from a canter into a brisk gallop. "We've got to keep up!"

The four members of The Saddle Club raced after Veronica and Danny. Stevie grinned as the wind whipped Belle's mane back toward her. This was fun! She just hoped that Veronica didn't realize too soon where her map was leading her—or wonder why The Saddle Club girls were the only other riders in sight.

They came to the fence marking the boundary of Pine Hollow's land. Stevie steadied Belle, slowing her to a fast canter. She leaned forward as the horse sprang over the gate, with Starlight half a pace ahead to the left and Topside and Derby half a pace behind to the right.

"*Wahooooo!*" Tessa yelled with joy as they all landed safely on the far side.

They were entering the woods now. The path was wide and smooth, but the girls slowed their horses to a trot nonetheless. Veronica and Danny had slowed down a little bit, too, and were visible through the sparse trees a dozen yards ahead.

Before long the trees thinned out even more, and a meadow carpeted in fresh green grass and tiny blue wildflowers spread before them. Only a low stile separated the path they were on from the field, and the girls' horses jumped it easily, one after the other. Danny was already halfway across the meadow, moving at a steady gallop. The Saddle Club urged their horses forward. They weren't really trying to keep up, but they didn't want to lose sight of Veronica, either. Otherwise it wouldn't be nearly as much fun when she reached the "finish line."

"This is great," Lisa called to her friends as the horses galloped eagerly after Danny.

Carole had just been thinking the same thing. The sun

was sinking toward the horizon, but there was still plenty of light left in the clear summer sky. Overhead, birds twittered and flew busily about their business, and in the woods all around the wildflower meadow spring peepers were just warming up for their evening song.

Carole took a deep breath, drinking in the scents of the outdoors mingled with the sharp odor of Starlight's sweat. There was just a whiff of mothballs mixed in with it, too, courtesy of the nightgown, which she had hiked up over her waist in order to ride more easily, and its matching yellow nightcap. But that didn't make things any less wonderful.

When they reached the woods again after jumping an X-shaped gate on the far side of the meadow, the girls slowed their horses. Once Starlight had settled into a smooth extended trot, Carole turned to her friends. "I was just trying to figure something out," she said, a little breathless from the fast-paced ride. "Do you think that very first steeplechase was anything like this?"

Lisa and Stevie laughed, glancing down at their costumes, but Tessa looked thoughtful. "I was wondering the same thing," she said. "I mean, I've ridden in my share of jumping races back home. But somehow, even though I'm way off in America where they hardly even know the meaning of steeplechasing"—she paused to grin teasingly at her friends—"somehow, this feels a lot more . . . I don't know, authentic maybe. It has the spirit of what a true, old-fashioned cross-country run must have been like, whether it was that race in County Cork or the original version of the Midnight Steeplechase."

The others couldn't argue with that, so they didn't try. They just went back to enjoying the ride.

After a couple of miles over hill and dale, Lisa could tell that they had almost reached their goal. "Let's speed up," she called to her friends.

They had been cantering to give their horses a break, but now they urged them into a gallop as they crossed another open meadow. Danny had just reentered a patch of woods at the far side, and they saw Veronica glance back at them over one shoulder. Even at this distance, they recognized the smug look on her face.

"She thinks she's got this race in the bag," Stevie reported with a grin. "Come on, let's go! We've got to make her think she's really earned it."

They managed to come within half a dozen yards of Danny's heels, but no closer. The big Thoroughbred gelding was too fast for the other horses. On the other side of the wooded patch, the landscape turned grassy and park-like, perfectly smooth and flat aside from a few shrubs and a line of tall, stately evergreens a quarter mile away.

Carole spied a pair of stone chimneys peeking out over the tops of the evergreen windbreak. She crossed her fingers on the reins, hoping that Veronica wouldn't notice the building and figure things out too soon. The Saddle

Club had no idea if she had actually managed to get herself invited to this particular house before . . .

The girls urged their horses forward even faster, jumping them over a narrow, meandering stream and then bursting through the windbreak into the Penningtons' front yard. Veronica had arrived seconds before them and had pulled Danny up, looking confused.

"Hey," she called, twisting around in her saddle to talk to the other girls, who had also pulled their horses to a stop. Veronica's sheep nightcap started to wobble as she turned, and she had to grab it to keep it on her hard hat. "What's the deal here?" she demanded irritably. "I thought someone said the finish line was some old wall in a field." She reached into her pocket for her map.

"Hang back here," Carole told her friends in a low voice. "We want to make sure she's the center of attention."

Her friends nodded and kept their horses in the long, late-day shadow of the evergreen windbreak.

A second later the front door of the old stone house banged open. "Hey!" Miles Pennington yelled, stepping out onto the porch. "Veronica? Is that you?"

"Cool," Stevie whispered to her friends. "I guess Miles believed me when I called and told him he and his friends might have an interesting visitor tonight during their party."

Veronica froze. Then she slowly looked up from her

map, a look of horror on her face. "M-Miles?" she stammered, grabbing for her nightcap. But at that moment several other teenage boys poured out of the house behind Miles, whooping and hollering. Even the usually unflappable Danny was startled by the sudden noise. He shied a few steps to one side, and Veronica had to grab for his mane to stay in the saddle. The sheep hat swayed woozily from side to side on her head. Her pink bunny top flapped in the breeze.

"Hey, guys!" Miles cried. "This is one of the girls who rides at the stable where Mother is keeping the team."

"Wow!" exclaimed a tall boy with a shock of blond hair and a mischievous grin. "People really know how to dress here in Virginia!"

Veronica's face was bright red. The other girls were feeling a little flushed, too, but only because they were laughing so hard. As the boys continued to laugh and point at Veronica and joke about her outfit—which she was in the process of ripping off and throwing angrily onto the ground—Tessa turned to her friends.

"I must say," she said between giggles, "it may not be very nice of me, but this really does make me feel a lot better."

Lisa grinned. "You know what the best part is?" She pointed.

The other girls looked and saw that the boys had surrounded Veronica. One of them was holding Danny by the bridle and looking him over admiringly. The tall blond boy had grabbed the discarded sheep hat and jammed it on his own head, laughing hysterically. Miles and a couple of the other boys had grabbed Veronica's map and were playing keep away with it while she shouted insults at them.

"What's the best part?" Carole asked Lisa curiously. "I honestly can't decide."

"They're destroying the evidence," Lisa replied simply. "Don't you see? That bogus map is the only thing she could use to prove we set this up." She shrugged and watched as the map fell into a patch of dirt. A second later, Danny shifted his weight and stepped on it, grinding it into the ground. "Now all we have to do is play dumb. She can't prove a thing. And when Max gets wind of that bet between her and Tessa . . ."

"Ah," Tessa said wisely. "Yes. We'll have to make sure that gets back to him somehow. Then he'll assume that Veronica is just being a sore loser."

Carole glanced over at Stevie. She was shaking her head.

"What is it?" Carole asked. "Don't you think that will work?"

"Oh, sure." Stevie waved her hand airily. "I wasn't disagreeing with that. I was disagreeing with what you said about the messed-up map being the best part. That's not the best part. The whole thing is the best part!" She grinned. "Revenge is sweet!"

Her friends couldn't help agreeing with that. They

turned to watch as Veronica tried to convince Miles's friends to let Danny go. She seemed very upset. Danny, however, didn't share her consternation. After his exhausting run through the countryside, he seemed perfectly willing to stand with the nice boy who was patting his neck as he held the bridle.

"Come on," Tessa said at last. She gathered Topside's reins. "We ought to get moving. Technically, we've still got to get to that stone wall before Veronica does, just in case she ever figures out where it really is."

The others nodded. "I know a shortcut," Stevie said. "We won't even have to canter. The horses could probably use a rest anyway."

"Definitely." Lisa patted Derby. It still didn't feel quite right being out there without Prancer, but the big chestnut gelding was fun to ride, too. Whatever Stevie said, Lisa had her own opinion about the best part of this wacky midnight steeplechase. It had reassured her that she and Derby really could work well together. That made her think that the next week's point-to-point could be a lot of fun.

Carole had her own ideas about the best part of the evening, too. She loved the fact that they had been able to combine their revenge plan with an exhilarating evening ride through the countryside. She was sure that was why their plan had been so successful—because anything just seemed to work out better when there were horses around. Although water balloons occasionally had their place too, of course . . .

There was no doubt in Stevie's mind about the best part of the evening. As the four friends rode through the windbreak, she couldn't resist taking one last peek at Veronica. Her grin stretched even wider when she saw that Miles had managed to jump up and jam the now muddy sheep hat back onto Veronica's head just as Mrs. Pennington emerged onto the front porch. The expression of surprise on the regal old woman's face and the look of dismay on Veronica's were the icing on the cake as far as Stevie was concerned.

No, there was no doubt in her mind at all. "Revenge is sweet," she whispered again as she urged Belle forward after her friends.

"IT'S HARD TO BELIEVE that such big horses can turn so smoothly," Carole commented the next afternoon. "Especially when they're dragging that pony cart around behind them."

The four members of The Saddle Club were leaning on the fence of the outdoor ring, watching as Mrs. Pennington exercised her team of Cleveland Bays. Her own carriages still hadn't arrived from Pennsylvania, so she was borrowing Max's pony cart. Hodge and Podge were pulling it easily around the large ring, following their driver's every command.

Stevie was impressed with the team's actions, too. But she was more interested in rehashing the events of the evening before. "So Veronica must have spent an hour trying to convince Max that we tricked her," she exulted.

"You could tell he was pretty suspicious, though," Lisa reminded Stevie, shading her eyes from the sun as she turned to look at her. "We're just lucky he overheard Britt and Polly talking about that bet Tessa and Veronica made."

"It was a close call," Tessa agreed. "I'm just glad we got away with it—for your sakes." She grinned. "And for mine. I'd be awfully bored riding here at Pine Hollow for the next week without the lot of you."

"Ha-ha," Stevie said sarcastically. She glanced over her shoulder at the stable building and sighed. "Still, I wish this probation would end. It's kind of stressful to have to be so good all the time." She looked surprised when her friends all burst out laughing. Then she realized that what she had said actually was kind of funny, all things considered, so she laughed, too.

Tessa was the first one to get serious again. "It's good that we can joke about it," she said. "But I still feel rather guilty. If it weren't for me, Veronica wouldn't have as easy a time torturing you. I'm like a walking target."

Lisa shrugged. "That's not your fault. Veronica is the one with the problem, not you. I'm just sorry you let her off the hook for your bet."

"Me too," Stevie put in. "I was looking forward to seeing her as a rodeo clown at the parade. I was going to call the mayor and everything." She heaved a disappointed sigh.

"Sorry, Stevie." Tessa chuckled. "I thought canceling the bet was the gracious thing to do. After all, we already got our reward." She shrugged. "And call me mad, but Veronica seemed a little friendlier after I did it."

"You're mad," Stevie said promptly. "At least, if by *mad* you mean 'crazy.' If Veronica seemed friendly, you can be sure it was because she thought someone important was watching."

"Let me have my dreams," Tessa joked. "I'm hoping that if I can get Veronica feeling less hostile to me, I won't feel like my very presence puts you in constant danger of losing your riding privileges."

Stevie shrugged. "Give up that dream right now. Veronica will never change. She's the one who got you kicked out of the junior hurdle, remember?"

Tessa rolled her eyes. "Don't remind me," she said. "I still wish I could ride in it, especially after last night. Topside could leave you all in the dust!" She shrugged. "But I'll survive."

Lisa grinned and slung an arm around Tessa's shoulders. "Would it make you feel better if we took you on an extra-special Saddle Club trail ride?"

Tessa stuck out her tongue. "Silly. We were planning to do that anyway."

"I know," Lisa replied. "But that was just an ordinary trail ride. This is an extra-special one."

Carole nodded. "And that makes all the difference."

166

What happens to The Saddle Club next?
Read Bonnie Bryant's exciting new series
and find out.

High school. Driver's licenses. Boyfriends. Jobs.

A lot of new things are happening, but one thing remains the same: Stevie Lake, Lisa Atwood, and Carole Hanson are still best friends. However, even among best friends some things do change, and problems can strain any friendship . . . but these three can handle it. Can't they?

Read an excerpt from Pine Hollow #1: *The Long Ride.*

PROLOGUE

"DO YOU THINK we'll get there in time?" Stevie Lake asked, looking around for some reassuring sign that the airport was near.

"Since that plane almost landed on us, I think it's safe to say that we're close," Carole Hanson said.

"Turn right here," said Callie Forester from the backseat.

"And then left up ahead," Carole advised, picking out directions from the signs that flashed past near the airport entrance. "I think Lisa's plane is leaving from that terminal there."

"Which one?"

"The one we just passed," Callie said.

"Oh," said Stevie. She gripped the steering wheel tightly and looked for a way to turn around without causing a major traffic tie-up.

"This would be easier if we were on horseback," said Carole.

"Everything's easier on horseback," Stevie agreed.

"Or if we had a police escort," said Callie.

"Have you done that?" Stevie asked, trying to maneuver the car across three lanes of traffic.

"I have," said Callie. "It's kind of fun, but dangerous. It makes you think you're almost as important as other people tell you you are."

Stevie rolled her window down and waved wildly at the confused drivers around her. Clearly, her waving confused them more, but it worked. All traffic stopped. She crossed the necessary three lanes and pulled onto the service road.

It took another ten minutes to get back to the right and then ten more to find a parking place. Five minutes into the terminal. And then all that was left was to find Lisa.

"Where do you think she is?" Carole asked.

"I know," said Stevie. "Follow me."

"That's what we've been doing all morning," Callie said dryly. "And look how far it's gotten us."

But she followed anyway.

ALEX LAKE REACHED across the table in the airport cafeteria and took Lisa Atwood's hand.

"It's going to be a long summer," he said.

Lisa nodded. Saying good-bye was one of her least favorite activities. She didn't want Alex to know how hard it was, though. That would just make it tougher on him. The two of them had known each other for four years—as long as Lisa had been best friends with Alex's twin sister, Stevie. But they'd only started dating six months earlier. Lisa could hardly believe that. It seemed as if she'd been in love with him forever.

"But it is just for the summer," she said. The words sounded dumb even as they came out of her mouth. The summer *was* long. She wouldn't come back to Virginia until right before school started.

"I wish your dad didn't live so far away, and I wish the summer weren't so long."

"It'll go fast," said Lisa.

"For you, maybe. You'll be in California, surfing or something. I'll just be here, mowing lawns."

"I've never surfed in my life—"

"Until now," said Alex. It was almost a challenge, and Lisa didn't like it.

"I don't want to fight with you," said Lisa.

"I don't want to fight with you, either," he said, relenting. "I'm sorry. It's just that I want things to be different. Not very different. Just a little different."

"Me too," said Lisa. She squeezed his hand. It was a way to keep from saying anything else, because she was afraid that if she tried to speak she might cry, and she hated it when she cried. It made her face red and puffy, but most of all, it told other people how she was feeling. She'd found it useful to keep her feelings to herself these days. Like Alex, she wanted things to be different, but she wanted them to be very different, not just a little. She sighed. That was slightly better than crying.

"I TOLD YOU SO," said Stevie to Callie and Carole.

Stevie had threaded her way through the airport terminal, straight to the cafeteria near the security checkpoint. And there, sitting next to the door, were her twin brother and her best friend.

"Surprise!" the three girls cried, crowding around the table.

"We just couldn't let you be the only one to say goodbye to Lisa," Carole said, sliding into the booth next to Alex.

"We had to be here, too. You understand that, don't you?" Stevie asked Lisa as she sat down next to her.

"And since I was in the car, they brought me along," said Callie, pulling up a chair from a nearby table.

"You guys!" said Lisa, her face lighting up with joy. "I'm so glad you're here. I was afraid I wasn't going to see you for months and months!"

She *was* glad they were there. It wouldn't have felt right if she'd had to leave without seeing them one more time. "I thought you had other things to do."

"We just told you that so we could surprise you. We did surprise you, didn't we?"

"You surprised me," Lisa said, beaming.

"Me too," Alex said dryly. "I'm surprised, too. I really thought I could go for an afternoon, just *one* afternoon of my life, without seeing my twin sister."

Stevie grinned. "Well, there's always tomorrow," she said. "And that's something to look forward to, right?"

"Right," he said, grinning back.

Since she was closest to the outside, Callie went and got sodas for herself, Stevie, and Carole. When she rejoined the group, they were talking about everything in the world except the fact that Lisa was going to be gone for the summer and how much they were all going to miss one another.

She passed the drinks around and sat quietly at the end of the table. There wasn't much for her to say. She didn't really feel as if she belonged there. She wasn't anybody's best friend. It wasn't as if they minded her being there, but she'd come along because Stevie had offered to drive her to a tack shop after they left the airport. She was simply along for the ride.

". . . And don't forget to say hello to Skye."

"Skye? Skye who?" asked Alex.

"Don't pay any attention to him," Lisa said. "He's just jealous."

"You mean because Skye is a movie star?"

"And say hi to your father and the new baby. It must be exciting that you'll meet your sister."

"Well, of course, you've already met her, but now she's crawling, right? It's a whole different thing."

An announcement over the PA system brought their chatter to a sudden halt.

"It's my flight," Lisa said slowly. "They're starting to board and I've got to get through security and then to Gate . . . whatever."

"Fourteen," Alex said. "It comes after Gate Twelve. There are no thirteens in airports."

"Let's go."

"Here, I'll carry that."

"And I'll get this one . . ."

As Callie watched, Lisa hugged Carole and Stevie. Then she kissed Alex. Then she hugged her friends again. Then she turned to Alex.

"I think it's time for us to go," Carole said tactfully.

"Write or call every day," Stevie said.

"It's a promise," said Lisa. "Thanks for coming to the airport. You, too, Callie."

Callie smiled and gave Lisa a quick hug before all the girls backed off from Lisa and Alex.

Lisa waved. Her friends waved and turned to leave her alone with Alex. They were all going to miss her, but the girls had one another. Alex only had his lawns to mow. He needed the last minutes with Lisa.

"See you at home!" Stevie called over her shoulder, but she didn't think Alex heard. His attention was completely focused on one person.

Carole wiped a tear from her eye once they'd rounded a corner. "I'm going to miss her."

"Me too," said Stevie.

Carole turned to Callie. "It must be hard for you to understand," she said.

"Not really," said Callie. "I can tell you three are really close."

"We are," Carole said. "Best friends for a long time. We're practically inseparable." Even to her the words sounded exclusive and uninviting. If Callie noticed, she didn't say anything.

The three girls walked out of the terminal and found their way to Stevie's car. As she turned on the engine, Stevie was aware of an uncomfortable empty feeling. She really didn't like the idea of Lisa's being gone for the summer, and her own unhappiness was not going to be helped by a brother who was going to spend the entire time moping about his missing girlfriend. There had to be something that would make her feel better.

"Say, Carole, do you want to come along with us to the tack shop?" she asked.

"No, I can't," Carole said. "I promised I'd bring in the horses from the paddock before dark, so you can just drop me off at Pine Hollow. Anyway, aren't you due at work in an hour?"

Stevie glanced at her watch. Carole was right. Everything was taking longer than it was supposed to this afternoon.

"Don't worry," Callie said quickly. "We can go to the tack shop another time."

"You don't mind?" Stevie asked.

"No. I don't. Really," said Callie. "I don't want you to be late for work—either of you. If my parents decide to get a pizza for dinner again, I'm going to want it to arrive on time!"

Stevie laughed, but not because she thought anything was very funny. She wasn't about to forget the last time she'd delivered a pizza to Callie's family. In fact, she wished it hadn't happened, but it had. Now she had to find a way to face up to it.

As she pulled out of the airport parking lot, a plane roared overhead, rising into the brooding sky. *Maybe that's Lisa's plane*, she thought. The noise of its flight seemed to mark the beginning of a long summer.

The first splats of rain hit the windshield as Stevie paid their way out of the parking lot. By the time they were on the highway, it was raining hard. The sky had darkened to a steely gray. Streaks of lightning brightened it, only to be followed by thunder that made the girls jump.

The storm had come out of nowhere. Stevie flicked on the windshield wipers and hoped it would go right back to nowhere.

The sky turned almost black as the storm strengthened.

Curtains of rain ripped across the windshield, pounding on the hood and roof of the car. The wipers flicked uselessly at the torrent.

"I hope Fez is okay," said Callie. "He hates thunder, you know."

"I'm not surprised," said Carole, trying to control her voice. It seemed to her that there were a lot of things Fez hated. He was as temperamental as any horse she had ever ridden.

Fez was one of the horses in the paddock. Carole didn't want to upset Callie by telling her that. If she told Callie he'd been turned out, Callie would wonder why he hadn't just been exercised. If she told Callie she'd exercised him, Callie might wonder if he was being overworked. Carole shook her head. What was it about this girl that made Carole so certain that whatever she said, it would be wrong? Why couldn't she say the one thing she really needed to say?

Still, Carole worked at Pine Hollow, and that meant taking care of the horses that were boarding there—and that meant keeping the owners happy.

"I'm sure Fez will be fine. Ben and Max will look after him," Carole said.

"I guess you're right," said Callie. "I know he can be difficult. Of course, you've ridden him, so you know that, too. I mean, that's obvious. But it's spirit, you see. Spirit is the key to an endurance specialist. He's got it, and I think he's got the makings of a champion. We'll work together this summer, and come fall . . . well, you'll see."

Spirit—yes, it was important in a horse. Carole knew

that. She just wished she understood why it was that Fez's spirit was so irritating to her. She'd always thought of herself as someone who'd never met a horse she didn't like. Maybe it was the horse's owner . . .

"Uh-oh," said Stevie, putting her foot gently on the brake. "I think I got it going a little too fast there."

"You've got to watch out for that," Callie said. "My father says the police practically lie in wait for teenage drivers. They love to give us tickets. Well, they certainly had fun with me."

"You got a ticket?" Stevie asked.

"No, I just got a warning, but it was almost worse than a ticket. I was going four miles over the speed limit in our hometown. The policeman stopped me, and when he saw who I was, he just gave me a warning. Dad was furious—at me and at the officer, though he didn't say anything to the officer. He was angry at him because he thought someone would find out and say I'd gotten special treatment! I was only going four miles over the speed limit. Really. Even the officer said that. Well, it would have been easier if I'd gotten a ticket. Instead, I got grounded. Dad won't let me drive for three months. Of course, that's nothing compared to what happened to Scott last year."

"What happened to Scott?" Carole asked, suddenly curious about the driving challenges of the Forester children.

"Well, it's kind of a long story," said Callie. "But—"

"Wow! Look at that!" Stevie interrupted. There was an amazing streak of lightning over the road ahead. The dark afternoon brightened for a minute. Thunder followed instantly.

"Maybe we should pull off the road or something?" Carole suggested.

"I don't think so," said Stevie. She squinted through the windshield. "It's not going to last long. It never does when it rains this hard. We get off at the next exit anyway."

She slowed down some more and turned the wipers up a notch. She followed the car in front of her, keeping a constant eye on the two red spots of the car's taillights. She'd be okay as long as she could see them. The rain pelted the car so loudly that it was hard to talk. Stevie drove on cautiously.

Then, as suddenly as it had started, the rain stopped. Stevie spotted the sign for their exit, signaled, and pulled off to the right and up the ramp. She took a left onto the overpass and followed the road toward Willow Creek.

The sky was as dark as it had been, and there were clues that there had been some rain there, but nothing nearly as hard as the rain they'd left on the interstate. Stevie sighed with relief and switched the windshield wipers to a slower rate.

"I think I'll drop you off at Pine Hollow first," she said, turning onto the road that bordered the stable's property.

Pine Hollow's white fences followed the contour of the road, breaking the open, grassy hillside into a sequence of paddocks and fields. A few horses stood in the fields, swishing their tails. One bucked playfully and ran up a hill, shaking his head to free his mane in the wind. Stevie smiled. Horses always seemed to her the most welcoming sight in the world.

"Then I'll take Callie home," Stevie continued, "and

after that I'll go over to Pizza Manor. I may be a few minutes late for work, but who orders pizza at five o'clock in the afternoon anyway?"

"Now, now," teased Carole. "Is that any way for you to mind your Pizza Manors?"

"Well, at least I have my hat with me," said Stevie. Or did she? She looked into the rearview mirror to see if she could spot it, and when that didn't do any good, she glanced over her shoulder. Callie picked it up and started to hand it to her.

"Here," she said. "We wouldn't want— Wow! I guess the storm isn't over yet!"

The sky had suddenly filled with a brilliant streak of lightning, jagged and pulsating, accompanied by an explosion of thunder.

It startled Stevie. She shrieked and turned her face back to the road. The light was so sudden and so bright that it blinded her for a second. The car swerved. Stevie braked. She clutched at the steering wheel and then realized she couldn't see because the rain was pelting even harder than before. She reached for the wiper control, switching it to its fastest speed.

There was something to her right! She saw something move, but she didn't know what it was.

"Stevie!" Carole cried.

"Look out!" Callie screamed from the backseat.

Stevie swerved to the left on the narrow road, hoping it would be enough. Her answer was a sickening jolt as the car slammed into something solid. The car spun around, smashing against the thing again. When the thing screamed, Stevie knew it was a horse. Then it disappeared from her field of vision. Once again, the car spun. It smashed against the guardrail on the left side of the road and tumbled up and over it as if the rail had never been there.

Down they went, rolling, spinning. Stevie could hear the screams of her friends. She could hear her own voice, echoing in the close confines of the car, answered by the thumps of the car rolling down the hillside into a gully. Suddenly the thumping stopped. The screams were stilled. The engine cut off. The wheels stopped spinning. And all Stevie could hear was the idle *slap, slap slap* of her windshield wipers.

"Carole?" she whispered. "Are you okay?"

"I think so. What about you?" Carole answered.

"Me too. Callie? Are you okay?" Stevie asked.

There was no answer.

"Callie?" Carole echoed.

The only response was the girl's shallow breathing.

How could this have happened?

ABOUT THE AUTHOR

Bonnie Bryant is the author of nearly a hundred books about horses, including The Saddle Club series, Saddle Club Super Editions, and the Pony Tails series. She has also written novels and movie novelizations under her married name, B. B. Hiller.

Ms. Bryant began writing The Saddle Club in 1986. Although she had done some riding before that, she intensified her studies then and found herself learning right along with her characters Stevie, Carole, and Lisa. She claims that they are all much better riders than she is.

Ms. Bryant was born and raised in New York City. She still lives there, in Greenwich Village, with her two sons.

Don't miss Bonnie Bryant's companion novel
to *English Horse* . . .

ENGLISH RIDER
The Saddle Club #80

Tessa and Veronica best friends? That's the way it looks. Instead of hanging out with The Saddle Club, their visiting English friend, Lady Theresa, is spending all her time with Veronica diAngelo. They talk together, shop together, and even ride together. Veronica is thrilled and can already see herself being invited back to England to meet Tessa's cousins—the royal family. Stevie, Carole, and Lisa are confused and upset. Have they lost one of their best friends to their worst enemy?

Have Veronica and Tessa buried the hatchet? Or is something else going on?

Don't miss Bonnie Bryant's next exciting Saddle Club
adventure . . .

WAGON TRAIL
The Saddle Club #81

The Saddle Club is heading west—on the Oregon Trail.
They're taking part in a re-creation of the famous
wagon train ride across the American West. Things may
be a little easier for these modern-day pioneers, but they
still have their fair share of problems. Stevie has to
drive their wagon—and wear a dress! She isn't sure
which is worse. Lisa has to contend with a reluctant
cow that *really* doesn't want to walk across the prairie.
Even Carole is finding the long days in the saddle a
little more than she bargained for.

This exciting story continues in *Quarter Horse*, The
Saddle Club #82.